"Superb suspense, deft unraveling, and skillful character dismantling."

—*Chicago Sunday Tribune*

"Sleek and satisfactory."

—*New York Herald Tribune Book Review*

"Lovely job of back-tracking of clues."

—*San Francisco Chronicle*

BLACK WIDOW was filmed in 1954 by Nunnally Johnson and starred Van Heflin, Ginger Rogers, Gene Tierney, Peggy Ann Garner, George Raft, and Reginald Gardiner.

Mysteries by
PATRICK QUENTIN
Featuring Peter Duluth

PUZZLE FOR FOOLS
PUZZLE FOR PLAYERS*
PUZZLE FOR PUPPETS*
PUZZLE FOR WANTONS
PUZZLE FOR FIENDS
PUZZLE FOR PILGRIMS
RUN TO DEATH*
BLACK WIDOW*

*available in a library of Crime Classics® edition

PATRICK QUENTIN

BLACK WIDOW

A Peter Duluth Mystery

LIBRARY OF CRIME CLASSICS®

MISTER E'S™

INTERNATIONAL POLYGONICS, LTD.
NEW YORK CITY

BLACK WIDOW

Copyright © 1952 by Patrick Quentin.

Library of Congress Card Catalog # 91-73849
ISBN 1-55882-111-2

Printed and manufactured in the United States of America.
First IPL printing October 1991.
10 9 8 7 6 5 4 3 2 1

CHAPTER ONE

I met Nanny Ordway at one of Lottie Marin's parties. It was a very ordinary beginning for an episode that dragged us all into disaster. My wife had taken her mother to Jamaica to recover from a gall-bladder operation, and I had too much work on hand to go with them. That same day, around midnight after the show, Lottie Marin called from upstairs.

"Come on up, Peter. There's a party."

I didn't want to go to a party or to encourage Lottie Marin's obvious determination to organize me as a grass-widower. But I was missing Iris, and the apartment, which reminded me of her at every turn, wasn't helping. I thought: I might as well go up just for a while.

So I went.

Lottie's apartment, which was immediately above our own, was full of assorted guests, the way it always was on Saturday nights. I didn't notice Nanny Ordway for quite a while. She wasn't at all a conspicuous person.

"Peter, darling!" Lottie came to the door for me herself. "I knew you'd be lonely. I knew you'd just be sitting there moping for Iris."

Lottie and I had known each other around the Theater for years. But recently, since she and her husband had become our neighbors and I had produced and directed her latest show, *Star Rising*, she had developed one of her sudden and celebrated infatuations for Iris and myself. Most people in the Theater, although Lottie was a great star and a world-wide celebrity, avoided intimacy with her because she was nosy, bossy and insufferably demanding. But Iris and I had put up with her bullying crush not only because I had to work with her but because we were both, in a funny way, fond of her. She was a bitch and a bore, but she didn't mean to be. She just terribly wanted to be liked and had never learned how to be likable. That was her trouble.

That night she was wearing a very grand white evening dress which made her look as if she were just about to be presented to the Court of St. James, or rather as if the Court of St. James was just about to be presented to her. She never hit the right clothes for the right occasion. That was a hangover, perhaps, from Oatfields, Wisconsin, which, although she kept it a dark secret, had been her birthplace.

"Darling, Alec Ryder's just in from London. He saw *Star Rising* tonight and he adored me. He's dying to talk to you. Come on. Brian will fix you a drink." She looped her arm through mine, giving me a meaning glance from that peculiar, memorable face which caricatured so effectively in the Theater Section of the Sunday *Herald Tribune*. "At least—I suppose you are drinking tonight, aren't you?"

That was one of those irritating remarks for which Lottie had a genius. She knew that, years ago, before I met Iris, I had gone off the rails after my first wife's death. I had drunk much too much and ended up in a nervous breakdown. At the time of my cure the doctors had told me I should never drink when I was depressed. It was something everyone else had forgotten. But Lottie remembered, and now she was dragging it out to show what an old friend she was, how sympathetic and understanding.

I snapped, "Why the hell shouldn't I be drinking, Lottie?"

She squeezed my hand. "You know best, darling, of course. I was just a little worried. That's all."

She took me to a bar where Brian Mullen, her latest and most successful husband, was mixing drinks. The bar was all chromium and blond wood and had been given to her by a Television sponsor. Brian grinned at me.

"Hi, Peter. Be right with you. Have to take a lemonade to a forlorn little female in a corner."

He carried the lemonade to a girl who was sitting alone by the window. That girl was Nanny Ordway, but I didn't know it at the time. I hardly glanced at her.

Brian came back and got me a drink. Lottie brought Alec Ryder over. Alec Ryder was a very successful and smooth English playwright married to one of London's brightest young theatrical stars. He said all the right things about Lottie and *Star Rising*, and Lottie started to purr like an ocelot with its spine tickled.

She purred less when Alec Ryder told us why he had flown to New York. He had just finished a new play and was looking for an American actress to do the lead in London. He thought my wife, who was an actress too, would be perfect in the part. Did I think she might be interested?

Almost before the words were out of his mouth, Lottie broke in, "Darling, it's quite impossible. Iris has decided to take a year's vacation."

That was perfectly true. But Lottie had no right to say it. I should have said it.

"Yes, darling," she continued, "Iris is just going to be Mrs. Duluth for a whole year. You know how crazy she and Peter are about each other. Just like Brian and me."

Some blonde actress whom I vaguely recognized had come over and was talking to Brian. When Lottie had a couple of drinks in her, she always got possessive about her husband. Now she neatly edged between him and the actress and twined her arms around his neck. I knew what the routine would be next. We'd get a speech about how perfectly mated she and Brian were and how second-best perfectly mated were Iris and I. The easy-going Brian never seemed to mind, but I didn't feel in the mood. I pretended to see someone I knew and drifted away.

Lottie had depressed me. Not only with her crass remark about drink but by her very Theaterness. Occasionally, only occasionally, I start hating the Theater with its narrow interests, its detachment from the rest of life, its passionate cult of itself. I decided that if I didn't find someone non-theatrical to talk to, I'd slip back down to the apartment and settle for loneliness.

I saw quite a few people I knew, but no one that fitted my mood. Gordon Ling, to whom I'd given a biggish part in *Star Rising*, flashed me a smile. But Gordon, too handsome at forty-five, too cheerful, too determined not to admit failure, was a most actorish actor. I knew he wanted to complain about a couple of lines of his I had cut at a recent run-through and I couldn't have faced him right then. I pretended I hadn't seen him and turned away, walking toward the window.

That's how I met Nanny Ordway. I hadn't the slightest intention of stopping to speak to her, but as I passed she put out her hand and surprisingly touched my arm.

"Won't you talk to me?" she said. "I don't think I'm terribly dull. Let's find out what you think."

I am always cautious with young girls I don't know. By bitter experience, I know that ninety out of a hundred of them think of a producer only as something on which to grind an axe. The most innocent greeting is usually the first step toward the casting office.

I paused and looked down at the girl sitting there in front of the expanse of undraped window below which the East River was glittering. She wasn't pretty or at all smartly dressed. Those were the first things I noticed. I noticed too that she was very young and she didn't seem to be wearing any make-up. She held a half-empty lemonade glass in her hand. I remembered Brian's remark then: *I'm fixing a lemonade for a forlorn little female in a corner.*

"I wish you'd sit down." Her voice was light and pleasant. "My mother always told me that a girl who couldn't get a man to talk to her after the first thirty minutes at a party might as well go out and shoot herself."

I liked her voice. I rather liked her face. It was intelligent and not trying to be anything it wasn't. Her hair was dark and she wore it in a page-boy bob with bangs. She was a little Greenwich Villagey, but then that made her so completely unlike Iris, and it was Iris' absence I was trying to forget.

I sat down next to her on the edge of the window seat. "Is your half-hour up yet?"

"You mean my half-hour for shooting myself? Oh, yes, long ago. No one's talked to me at all. Some people brought me but they've gone off being glamorous. I hope you're not glamorous. I hope you're not an Important Figure like everyone else."

"Don't you like important figures?"

"I don't know. I suppose I should. But I've never met any before. I don't know what to do with them."

"You just tell them how important they are and they give little grunts of satisfaction."

"They do?" She turned to me, tucking her legs under her on the window seat. "You'd better tell me who you are. If you're important, I'd like to hear you grunt."

"My name's Peter Duluth," I said.

The blood flooded her cheeks. She was one of those girls who can look charming and embarrassed at the same time.

"My God!" she said.

"Why—my God?"

"You—you're a producer or something terribly grand in the Theater and you're married to Iris Duluth, aren't you?"

"That's right."

"I never realized . . . I mean, I wouldn't ever have . . . Iris Duluth is wonderful. She's the most beautiful, moving actress I've ever seen." She got up. "I'm sorry I was so brash."

"My dear girl, I'm not Stalin. You don't have to organize Youth Parades with banners— The Workers of the Fifth Fish-Packing Soviet of Odessa bring homage to Peter Duluth."

She sat down again and suddenly laughed.

"What are you laughing about now?"

"You. You're a fraud. I told you how important you were and you didn't give little grunts of satisfaction."

"That was the grunt in reverse. The modest grunt. The really-I'm-not-anything-special-just-a-person response. Who are you?"

The smile, slightly sardonic now, was still in her eyes. "I'm not anything special. Just a person."

"In the Theater?"

"Heavens—no."

"That's a relief. What do you do?"

"I get up. I eat. I go to bed."

"No visible means of support?"

6

"Not very visible. Really, I suppose, I'm a writer. I haven't got anything published yet. I don't think I'm very good."

"How old are you?"

"Nineteen. No, that's a lie. I'm twenty. I try to pretend I'm not in the twenties because in the twenties you're supposed to have done something."

Until then, I'd started to forget what a kid she was. You have to be terribly young to make a remark like that. I was feeling less depressed.

"I know," I said. "Mozart wrote an opera when he was twelve."

"Well, it's true, isn't it?" she said almost angrily. "You can't just grow up. At least you've got to show talent."

"And you haven't shown any talent?"

"I don't think so. Sometimes it's terribly depressing."

"Isn't that lemonade terribly depressing? Have a drink."

"No, thank you. I don't drink. I used to. I gave it up. But if there's anything to eat . . . I'm simply starved."

"Lottie never serves food. Brian cooks her a great t-bone steak right after the performance. By the time the guests arrive, she isn't hungry any more."

I didn't know why I said that. It was unattractive and disloyal to disparage Lottie in front of a stranger. But this girl didn't seem like a stranger. Suddenly an idea came to me. I was bored with the party. I had been planning to leave anyway. The girl was hungry. Why shouldn't I take her out and give her something to eat? The scheme was a little exciting to me. It was so different from anything I would ever have dreamed of doing if Iris had been there—different enough to act as a tonic to my spirits. An innocent change of pace never harmed anyone.

I said, "Are you tired of this party?"

"No tireder than it is of me."

"Do you have to wait for the people you came with?"

"Mercy, no. They only brought me because they were stuck with me. They've probably left."

"Then how about coming out and getting something to eat?"

She said quickly, "But what about Iris Duluth—your wife?"

"She's away."

"Oh."

"You don't have to say Oh. I'm not one of those husbands who suddenly discover their wives don't understand them."

"You're very much in love with her, aren't you? One reads about it in columns."

"Yes, I'm very much in love with her."

She smiled then. "Fine. I'll come. I'd like it."

"What's your name?"

"Nanny," she said. "Nanny Ordway."

I didn't want the complication of saying goodnight to Lottie, but as we were making for the door, she came swooping over.

"Peter, you poor darling, I've been neglecting you." She stopped and looked penetratingly at Nanny Ordway. "Who's that?"

"That," I said, "is Miss Ordway. One of your guests. I'm taking her out to get something to eat. Then I'm going to bed. Say thanks to Brian for me. See you tomorrow."

Lottie stood quite still in her white dress that looked like the tent of some wealthy paladin at the Crusades.

"Well!" she said in her theater voice which can suggest a dozen simultaneous overtones. She gazed at the empty glass in my hand with all the anguish of a tender-hearted woman seeing her best friend galloping to perdition.

I could have killed her, but instead I kissed her.

8

"Goodnight, Lottie. Don't rock the boat."

When we were out in Sutton Place, Nanny Ordway slipped her arm through mine.

"She was furious. Charlotte Marin. Simply furious."

"Lottie only likes things she sponsors herself."

"To think of it! Charlotte Marin furious about me! That I should live to see the day."

I was wondering where to take her to eat at that hour, but she decided for me. There was a Hamburger Heaven on 55th at Madison, and we could walk. You get in a rut in the Theater. You end up feeling you have to go somewhere expensive, and you take taxis. It was warm for October and refreshing to be walking through the still-active Saturday night streets. Hamburger Heaven was very white and clean. We sat on barstools and ate hamburgers with coffee from thick china mugs. In the harsh illumination, with her dark hair flopping around her shoulders, Nanny Ordway looked even younger. Most very young girls make me feel decrepit at thirty-seven, but she didn't. I felt amused and kindly—and amused at myself. For over ten years my interests, my desires, my affections had been exclusively tied up with my wife. It was improbable that I should be out with a girl only a few hours after Iris' departure, but it seemed to be the right therapy.

"Better for the food?" I asked.

"Wonderful. Once I lived for six months on hamburgers."

"Didn't you get tired of them?"

"Oh, that was a lie again. Sometimes I ate hot-dogs." She turned on her stool, looking at me solemnly. "Have you ever been poor?"

"Not terribly."

"It's fun. It's almost like being in love. You wake up in the morning and you're yearning for something. You have the feeling: How long can I wait? You count the minutes till noon. And it isn't a man you're yearning for. It's a hamburger."

"Are you still poor?"

"Oh, yes."

"Live with parents?"

"No. I live alone. Kind of. With a girl from Boston." She put down her empty milk glass. "You're rich. Rich and in love. That must be fun too. But mostly the love part. Isn't it?"

"It's fine."

She talked about Iris then. She had seen all her recent plays and quite a lot of her movies. She was intelligent and enthusiastic about her. It always pleased me to have Iris praised. Somehow Nanny Ordway bridged the gulf of Iris' absence. Instead of brooding about the fact that she was away, I started to think: It won't be long before she's back.

After she'd finished her coffee, Nanny Ordway got up. "Now I must go home."

"So soon?"

"Oh, yes. I have to be at my desk at nine every day."

"Mozart got up at six."

She laughed. "That's right. Kid me when I get pretentious. That's my trouble. I'm pretentious."

Outside on Madison Avenue, I started looking for a taxi, but she stopped me. Whoever took a taxi? she said. Hadn't I heard of the subway? I could walk her to the Lexington Avenue station. We talked all the way. She entertained me. I didn't want it to be over so quickly.

At the head of the subway stairs, she held out her hand. "Goodnight. You've taught me one thing. I do like Important Figures."

"And I like twenty-year-old girls who haven't Achieved Anything."

"Don't be silly. I'm just a whim. Goodnight."

She started down the stairs. I called after her impulsively:

"I can phone you?"

"I'm not in the book."

I could hear a train roaring into the station below me. "Then give me your number."

Without answering, Nanny Ordway hurried down the steps and disappeared. I stood a moment at the head of the stairs before I turned away.

As I walked home, New York seemed different. I smelt it, saw it, felt it, almost as if it were an unfamiliar city. I was conscious of all the life going on around me—people meeting and saying goodbye and arguing and making love. New York was a lot of Nanny Ordways. Through her, I had stepped for a moment out of my own restricted little circle.

When I got back to the apartment, a cablegram had been slipped under the door. I picked it up. It said:

ARRIVED SAFELY. MOTHER DOESN'T MISS GALL BLADDER. I MISS YOU. DON'T LET LOTTIE SWALLOW YOU. LOVE. IRIS

Without Iris, the bed seemed impersonal as a hotel bed. Wasn't it Swedenborg who had the theory that a man and his wife are two halves of the same soul? I drifted into sleep, feeling very much a half.

I had forgotten Nanny Ordway. At least, I thought I had.

CHAPTER TWO

I was awakened next morning around ten-thirty by the phone. It was Lottie.

"Peter, are you alone?"

"For heaven's sake, what else would I be?"

"That's good. Then come up. Breakfast is ready."

"Breakfast?"

"My dear, you can't just sit there and eat by yourself. Brian's fixing everything. Come right on up."

Soon Lottie would have me up there sleeping in the same bed with them.

"I'm not hungry," I said, fighting for my independence.

"You'd better be." Brian's cheerful voice sounded on the kitchen extension. "Scrambled eggs and sausages."

"But . . ."

"Nonsense," broke in Lottie. I could just see her at the other end of the phone making ferocious doodles all over the telephone pad the way she always did when she felt she was being crossed.

"If you're not here in five minutes, I'll come down and get you."

I yawned and was sufficiently awake to start missing Iris again. Iris was the one who could handle Lottie. When I argued with her, I only got mad and then Lottie sulked, became unendurable and caused havoc at the theater. Resignedly, I got out of bed, put on a robe and went upstairs.

Lottie was wearing a terrible pair of Chinese lounging pajamas—a tomato red blouse with pagodas on it and a pair of chartreuse pants. She was bouncy the way she always was in the mornings, as if she had a full day ahead and was raring to go. Brian had cleared away all traces of last night's party. Lottie pecked me on the cheek and dragged me into the kitchen.

Sundays, the daily woman who worked for both Lottie and us didn't show up. Lottie and Brian always ate breakfast in the kitchen because it made Lottie feel domestic. Feeling domestic, with Lottie, consisted of reading the Sunday papers messily all over the kitchen table while Brian cooked. When we went in, we found her husband, tall, amiable, and handsome in a yellow robe, bending over the stove scrambling eggs.

Brian was the luckiest thing that had ever happened to Lottie. She had discovered him when she did her only picture in Hollywood five years before. He was a Montana boy who had been in the Coast Guard during the war. He had all the standard male requirements except any visible ambition. He had played a few small parts in some of Lottie's successes and had done a little stage-managing. But Lottie really preferred to keep him at home as a private asset and he never objected. He seemed perfectly happy answering her fan mail, cooking for her, running errands, and reminding her how wonderful she was. Although he was entirely dependent upon Lottie financially, there was nothing objectionable about the situation. Everyone agreed that Brian should be permanently endowed by Equity for his great service to the Theater in keeping Lottie Marin contented.

The Sunday papers were scattered all over the kitchen. On the table, among the dishes, was the Theater Section of the *Times*. I saw the headline: *Charlotte Marin Reaches New Heights*. So Brooks Atkinson had taken a return trip to *Star Rising*. That was fine. It would jack up the already soaring box-office returns and keep Lottie good-tempered for a week.

"Another rave from Atkinson, darling. Brian, do hurry up with those eggs."

Lottie's appetite was always enormous when things were going well. She sat down at the table and watched me with that gimlet look of hers. I knew exactly what was on her Oatfields, Wisconsin, mind. It came out when we were all of us halfway through our eggs.

"Well, Peter, who was that girl?"

"What girl?" I asked innocently.

"That girl you sneaked away with from the party."

"Her name's Nanny Ordway. I told you."

"I never invited her. I never heard of her. Brian, did you?"

"Did I what, dear?" asked Brian from behind the Sports Section.

"Invite a girl called Nanny Ordway last night?"

"Nanny Ordway? Don't think I know her. Should I?"

"Some people brought her," I said.

"Who?" demanded Lottie.

"I don't know. She didn't say."

"Well, I wish people wouldn't do things like that." The gimlet glance was back boring into me. "What exactly did you do with her anyway?"

"I took her to Hamburger Heaven and talked about Iris. Then I took her to her subway."

"Well," said Lottie, one perfectly mated individual to another, "I suppose it was all right. But I do think it's rather peculiar—with Iris only gone a few hours."

"Better cable her," I said. "Return at once. Peter taken mistress."

"Don't be silly. Still, I don't think it was wise. When a man's been married over ten years, he's in a very dangerous phase. It's a well-known fact." She paused to let these words of wisdom sink in. "Are you going to see her again?"

"Sure. I just sent her away to get baked into a pie. Tonight I'm going to cut the pie and she's going to spring out naked except for a pair of orgiastic scarlet garters.

Lottie flushed and looked annoyed. "Brian, dear, do put down that dreary Sports Section and read what Brooks Atkinson wrote about me."

Lottie had it all figured that I was to spend the rest of the morning with them and then catch a Sunday matinee so as not to be lonely. But I managed to slip away around noon, saying I had scripts to read. It was true. I was looking for another play to do that season. That was one of the reasons, including a normal aversion to my mother-in-law, why I hadn't been able to go with Iris to Jamaica. I got through the afternoon reading bad manuscripts and wondering why so many hundreds of misguided people think they can write plays. Then I went out to dinner with Alec Ryder, who tried to sell me again on Iris doing his play in London. It was a mild enough Sunday. I went on missing Iris all the time and wrote to her about Alec's offer, knowing she'd turn it down. I had meant to mention Nanny Ordway in the letter, but by that time, after my session with Alec, I had forgotten her.

I didn't, in fact, think about Nanny Ordway until the mail came on Monday morning. One of the envelopes was addressed in a large, sprawling handwriting I didn't know. I opened it. Inside there was nothing but a little kid's circle and line drawing of a girl sitting at a telephone with a typed telephone number floating above her in a balloon.

I smiled when I saw it and took it with me to the of-

fice. I went every day to the office even though, half the
time, when I had no new play getting started, there
wasn't much to do because of Miss Mills. Miss Mills had
been with me ten years and took most of the chores off
me. She supervised the stenographers, answered most of
the mail, weeded out playscripts, got rid of the wrong
actors, charmed the right actors, and settled most of the
squabbles of the *Star Rising* company. Miss Mills played
it sour but she was mother to all the world.

I had a conference with her about a script she was
crazy for and I didn't like. Then I spent ten minutes or
so calming down Gordon Ling, the actor from *Star
Rising* who had been at Lottie's two nights before. He
had finally trapped me about the cuts I'd made in his
lines in the third act. "It doesn't feel right any more,
Peter. I can't get it across, honest. And I've nothing to
say when I walk back to the sofa." It was the same old
actor's complaint. If actors had their way, each of their
own speeches would be as long as *Paradise Lost* and the
other members of the cast would answer in monosylla-
bles. It wasn't hard for me to be firm with Gordon. He'd
been out of work a long time. I'd given him the job
largely through kindness and he knew it. I soon got rid
of him.

After he left, I was alone and I took Nanny Ordway's
drawing out of my pocket. It was a cute little picture,
and on an impulse I dialed the number. If Lottie hadn't
made such a fuss about her, I probably would never have
done it. But I remembered that "dangerous phase"
dogma and, I suppose, I wanted to prove how impreg-
nable I was.

A girl's voice answered. "Hello."

"Nanny Ordway?"

"Who's calling?" The voice sounded Bostonian and
severe. The roommate.

"Peter Duluth."

"Wait a moment, please."

Soon Nanny came on the phone. "Hello." It was nice to hear her. It brought back pleasant memories.

"Hello. I just thought I'd call to find out how inspiration was flowing."

"It's flowing okay, I guess."

"That was a cute picture. Giotto was fifteen when Cimabue found him drawing sheep."

"There's no need to kid me. I haven't been pretentious yet, have I?"

"Had your hamburger?"

"What hamburger?"

"The one you wake up yearning for."

"Oh, no. Not yet. Besides, I don't yearn for them now. That was last year."

It suddenly occurred to me that I had no lunch date. It would be amusing to see her and why shouldn't I? To hell with Lottie. "How about lunch?"

"I'm sorry. I have lots more work to do."

"Is that a lie?"

"Why a lie?"

"You're always saying something and then saying it's a lie."

"Oh, no. It's true. I can't possibly come to lunch. It's against my schedule."

"Dinner any better?"

She paused. "Do you really mean it?"

"Of course."

"Then if you'll do it my way. Come here. You've already fed me. I'll cook dinner for you. You should see."

"See what?"

"How unimportant figures live. Do you know the Village?"

"Bon Soir? The Vanguard?"

"Oh, no. Not that. The real Village. I'll show you. Come at seven."

"Fine."

She gave me the address and elaborate subway directions. Soon after Miss Mills came in.

"What have you been doing, Peter. You look furtive."

Did I look furtive? It was stupid. There was nothing to look furtive about. But I almost wished I hadn't called. I wrote a letter to Iris. It was, as usual, a love letter. In it, I said:

"I forgot to tell you I've already been wildly unfaithful. I took a twenty-year-old girl away from Lottie's party the other day and fed her hamburgers. Now I'm going to have dinner with her in the Village. She has bangs and plans to be a literary genius and thinks you're wonderful. Lottie already has me tabbed for adultery and a return to the bottle. Watch out . . ."

I arrived at Nanny Ordway's apartment on Charlton Street at seven o'clock.

She opened the door to me in an apron over the same dress she had worn at Lottie's party. She looked homely until she smiled. I was glad she hadn't tried to fix herself up for me and glad that I didn't find her attractive at all. The girl she roomed with was out, she said. I was to make myself comfortable in the living-room and not fuss her in the kitchen. The living-room was a bedroom too. There were two studio couches. The Bostonian roommate seemed to be a painter. The walls, painted dark oxford blue, were hung with rather surly still-life of a Braque-ish variety. There were other pictures stacked against the walls and an easel pushed into a corner. Books were lying around over everything—

lofty books: Santayana, Malraux's *Psychologie de L'Art,*
Jean Genet in French, and some Henry James. A bottle
of Chianti and a glass were on the cluttered coffee table
by a bunch of violets in a jelly jar.

It was all depressingly Bohemian and rather pathetic.
"Drink the wine," called Nanny from the kitchen.
"It's put there for you."

I felt physically uncomfortable and a little foolish. I
couldn't quite see any more what I was doing in a
twenty-year-old girl's apartment. I drank some of the
wine. Finally Nanny came in with a spaghetti dinner.
It wasn't terribly good. We ate it on separate ends of
the coffee table with Henry James slipping every now
and then into the meat sauce.

It would have been awful if it hadn't been for Nanny's
enthusiasm. She sat there next to me, her dark hair
falling over her young face, pleased about every minute
of it. She was paying me back. She was showing me a
way of life she thought I didn't know. She chattered in
her leaping, inconsequential way. I felt ashamed of being bored, ashamed too of my own unadmitted prudish-
ness. To Nanny Ordway a casual, asexual evening with
a man was obviously an accepted social phenomenon.
Although she objected, I helped her with the dishes in
the horrible little kitchen.

There was a phonograph in the living-room. She made
coffee and put on Welitch's records of the end of *Salomé*.
She listened with all her body as if the music had been
written especially for her. She didn't talk about herself
or her writing. She didn't even talk about me. She just
seemed to like my company.

Afterwards we went out to some neighborhood bars
—"the real Village." They were none of them very exciting. In fact, without Nanny, they would have seemed

sordid and raffish, full of faky "artistic" types. We even danced at one dim little joint with a three-piece hot orchestra. She didn't dance as well as Iris.

"You see?" she said, smiling up at me, proud as if she had given me the biggest kick of my life. "You don't have to be rich to have fun."

But I didn't really have fun. I was almost glad when she said she had to go home. She didn't invite me in. She just stood on the steps above the ashcans put out for the garbage truck and held out her hand.

"I'll remember tonight," she said.

"So will I."

"Oh, no, you won't. Why should you? But at least you've seen. Tell your wife when you write. It would amuse her."

That was the first time she had mentioned Iris all evening.

"I've already written about you," I said.

She smiled. She was delighted. "I'm glad." And then: "I think it's wonderful for a girl and a man to be friends."

"Sure."

"It *is* possible. People talk such nonsense."

She stood there with her door key in her hand. I thought of that cluttered room she had to go back to with her roommate probably washing nylons in the bathroom. I thought of all the millions of other city lives all over the world with their drabness, their anxieties, their hopes that would never materialize. I shouldn't have come. It hadn't got anyone anywhere.

"Goodbye, Peter."

"Goodbye, Nanny."

CHAPTER THREE

When I reached home, I dropped in on Lottie and Brian for a night-cap so that Lottie wouldn't be difficult. The show had gone well and she was in a sweet mood the way she sometimes was, quiet and affectionate. I was pleased to see her as something which belonged with my sort of life. I didn't mention Nanny and she didn't ask where I had been. We talked about Iris and I went to bed purged of my cosmic pity for struggling young girls.

About two weeks went by before I had anything more to do with Nanny Ordway. Then one morning around eleven Miss Mills came into my office.

"Peter, there's a girl out there who won't go away. She says you picked her up last night at Roseland and promised her a part in a road company of *Star Rising*. She says she's come to sign the contracts."

"She's crazy. What's her name?"

Miss Mills grimaced. "Gloria," she said. "Gloria O'Dream."

"For God's sake!"

"Peter, you didn't do anything charmingly boyish last night, did you?"

"Of course not. It's some kind of a gag. Well, let her in, I guess."

Nanny came in. After Miss Mills had shut the door on her, she crossed to my desk. She was wearing an old tweed coat and no hat. She had a manila envelope in her hand.

"Hello. That was meant to be funny—that about Roseland and Gloria O'Dream. I suppose it wasn't, was it?"

I didn't quite know how I felt. Mostly I think I was flustered about Miss Mills, who wasn't at all pixy.

Nanny looked around the office. "So big—so opulent. How peculiar that business, which is so dreary, has to go on in a pretty place. Shouldn't I have come? Is it bad? I was just passing. I saw the name up on the window—Peter Duluth."

She looked so worried that I smiled. "It's a pleasure. Sit down, Miss O'Dream. What's that envelope you've got?"

She sat down in a chair across the desk from me. "Oh, it's just a manuscript. I've been to pick it up at the *New Yorker*. They turned it down."

"That's too bad."

"They said it was okay to write like Truman Capote and okay to write like Somerset Maugham. But it wasn't okay to write like them both at once. I've got to work a lot yet. I know that. Years maybe before I'm any good."

I asked to see the manuscript but she wouldn't hear of it. I'd been a little worried that she'd come angling for a lunch date. It was a reprehensible thought on my part. Why the hell shouldn't the kid try for a free lunch once in a while? But I had maligned her. She didn't even give me the chance to invite her. She got up after a couple of minutes and said she had to go.

"I just came in because I was passing."

"I'm glad."

She turned at the door, the manila envelope pressed against her small breasts. "Is it silly if I ask you something?"

"Of course not. Go ahead."

"If ever you feel like it, call me. Oh, I don't want you to take me out. Nothing like that. There's no point. But between friends—I do like a link. Will you? Call, I mean?"

"Sure I will."

"Thank you. Thank you so much."

She was out of the office before I realized that I didn't want her to go.

Miss Mills came in.

"All settled, Peter?"

"It was just a gag."

Miss Mills looked at me cleverly. "Well, whimsy will never cease, I guess. What is she? The Fairy Heliotrope from the top of the Christmas tree?"

That was when I decided I wouldn't see Nanny Ordway again, that I wouldn't call to make a "link." I didn't know why I liked being with her, but the fact that I did seemed to make it obvious that it all should stop. It was a relationship which had started for no particular reason and had no particular future. Links forged between friends! That was all kid stuff. It didn't become me to step that far out of my age bracket. The whole thing was pointless for both of us.

I shouldn't be thinking in terms of "both of us" either.

That afternoon I stood in on the matinee of *Star Rising*. Lottie was magnificent. No one in the audience could have imagined her as the tiresome, busy little woman upstairs in the Chinese lounging pajamas. From then on I spent almost all my time with her and Brian —almost as if I needed her possessiveness as a protection.

I was writing to Iris every day and she was writing back. Her mother was being difficult, feeling much grander than any of the other women at the hotel. As soon as she was quite recovered and had made some friends, Iris would leave her there and fly home, she said. I found one of her letters waiting for me at home one evening about a week later. I had been with Lottie and Brian to some party. I had drunk quite a bit and was feeling no pain.

I took Iris' letter to bed with me. In it, I read:

> "How are you getting along with your infant prodigy? Does she have a spaniel hair-do like George Eliot? I can imagine you sitting on studio couches in a smoke-filled attic, playing Dr. Sitwell on a phonograph you have to wind up with a handle. Go on with it, darling. It'll do you good to get a little female companionship that isn't Lottie. I have a wonderful British colonel with white mustaches down to his navel who shouts, 'Good show, what?' whenever I get a backhand over the tennis net. . . ."

I'm sure, if it hadn't been for that letter and if I hadn't been a little high, I would never have called Nanny Ordway. But I did. I reached over for the phone and dialed, feeling amused and paternal. It was late, but she answered almost at once.

"Hello."

"Hello, Miss O'Dream. I'm just forging a link."

"Oh, Mr. Du . . . Peter, hello."

"It's disgracefully late."

"No, it isn't. I've been sitting here writing."

"Truman Capote or Somerset Maugham?"

"I don't know. Both together again, I guess. It's so nice of you to call. You didn't have to."

"Are you alone?"

"Yes, I'm alone. Sort of. My roommate's asleep."

I could picture her at the other end of the phone,

24

curled up on one of the studio couches, her hair flopping over her face, her toe, maybe, kicking Santayana. Suddenly it all seemed so pleasant, so harmless—like Iris' white-mustached colonel.

"Good show, what?" I said.

"What, Peter? What did you say?"

"Nothing. I just called."

"I'm glad."

I thought of the dreary little room, the lingering kitchen smells from supper. Suddenly my cosmic feeling of pity, a little maudlin from liquor, was back.

"How about dinner tomorrow? You showed me the Village. I'll show you how the stinking rich live. Only fair, isn't it?"

She didn't answer for a while. I felt absurdly scared she would have a date.

At last she said, "Peter, do you really mean it?"

"Of course I mean it."

"I don't think you do. If you do, call me again in the morning."

"Nanny . . ."

"Goodnight, Peter. Pleasant dreams."

She hung up on me. I went to sleep. She was the first thing I thought of when I woke up in the morning. I felt embarrassed. I'd been a bit high when I called her and she'd suspected it. She wasn't going to believe in my dinner invitation unless I called again. In the matter-of-fact light of morning, my ignoble, patronizing impulse of the night before had vanished. I didn't want to have dinner with her at all. But now if I didn't call back, she would know I'd been tight and irresponsible. She'd be hurt. I lay in bed looking at the phone as if it were a dentist. Finally I called her and confirmed the date. She was to come to my place at seven.

I went upstairs then to have breakfast with Lottie and

Brian. Breakfast had become a ritual. The daily woman served all three of us in the bedroom. I sat on the side of the bed while Lottie and Brian stayed put.

Lottie gave me one of her gimlet looks.

"Peter, darling, you didn't drink too much last night, did you?"

"No, why?"

"You look funny." She turned to her sleepy, tousled husband. "Doesn't Peter look funny, Brian?"

I had some business to settle with the Guild that afternoon. It was six-fifteen before I realized I would be later than I thought. I called Nanny but there was no answer. I felt unreasonably anxious about it. It was almost seven-twenty when I got back to the apartment. Nanny Ordway was sitting cross-legged on the floor outside my front door. She had the old tweed coat over her arm but she was wearing an evening dress—a pale blue strapless affair.

"I'm terribly sorry," I said. "I called to let you know I'd be late but you'd already left."

She got up, smiling. "I imagined it was something like that." She twisted around in front of me. "Will this do? I don't own an evening dress. I borrowed it from my roommate. People do wear evening dresses, don't they, when they go to grand places, or is it only in the movies?"

The dress was all covered in little bows, the sort of thing a stuffy Boston debutante would have "come out" in several years ago at the Ritz. But she had a pretty neck and lovely shoulders. And somehow the wrongness of the dress touched me.

"You look fine," I said.

"Oh, well, it doesn't matter really."

I was getting out my key when Brian came running down the stairs from the floor above. When he saw us, he stopped dead.

"Hello, Peter." He glanced at Nanny. "Hello."

He looked awkward as if he'd caught me out in something I wouldn't want to be caught out in. "Lottie's gone off to the theater. I just thought we might have a drink. That is, if you weren't doing anything, I thought . . . but, never mind."

He started tactfully back up the stairs. I had a foolish impulse to call after him and ask him not to tell Lottie about Nanny. But I suppressed it. He'd tell Lottie anyway. He told her everything. If I asked him not to, it would just have been embarrassing for him and more compromising for me.

I let Nanny into the apartment. I was rather jittery and, forgetting she didn't drink, offered her a Martini. She said no thank you, she'd take a lemonade. I fixed the lemonade, put the phonograph on for her, and excused myself to shower and change.

When I came back into the living-room, she was sitting by the window, gazing out over the East River. She didn't hear me. I went up to her and put my hand on her shoulder. She turned quickly. Her eyes were shining.

"It's lovely—the room, the window. And the phonograph—it's wonderful. What nonsense I talked about being poor. If I lived here, I'd sit here by the window all day and I'd write. I'd write . . ."

"Like Truman Capote and Somerset Maugham."

"Oh, no. Not here. Here I could be myself. It's only that sometimes down in the Village, when you start to write, you feel you have to make everything more glamorous somehow—quite different—to counterbalance things. It wouldn't be like that. Not here."

I made myself a Martini. She walked around the room, examining everything, her long blue skirt rustling clumsily.

"That was Charlotte Marin's husband, wasn't it?"

"It was."

"Did he mind?"

"Mind?"

"About me. She—Charlotte Marin—minded at the party."

"There's nothing to mind about anyway."

"Of course there isn't. It's just that people . . . Are we really going somewhere expensive and glittering for dinner?"

"Anywhere you like."

She came toward me, holding out her hand solemnly. "Then I think I will have a cocktail, please."

We went to Voisin, which I don't normally do and can't normally afford. But now the evening had happened, I figured I might as well do it in style. She didn't seem to like it much although she was careful to praise everything. I think she had started to worry about her dress. I made her drink some wine and it did wonders. She got a little high, only a little, enough to stop feeling awed. She was really very intelligent. She missed nothing. It was extraordinary what good company she was. We lingered over dinner and then we went to the Ruban Bleu. We left quite early—about one-thirty and we were near home. It seemed quite natural to ask her home for a nightcap. She said: Yes, she'd come if we could play Welitch's *Salomé*. I had it, she knew. She'd seen it on the shelf. Her roommate's phonograph was being repaired and she'd missed it so much.

We played the Welitch *Salomé*. I didn't want to give it much volume because it was late. But the jangled, disturbing music filled the apartment. She listened, rapt, the way she had done in her own apartment. When it was over, she said:

"That's the way I would like to write. Just like that. That sort of mood." She paused and then quoted softly:

"*Das Geheimnis der Liebe is grüsser als das Geheimnis des Tod.* It's corny, maybe, but if you could do it right in a story!"

"Translate."

"The secret of love," she said, "is greater than the secret of death."

She looked so young and solemn that I grinned. "Treated à la Somerset Capote."

"Don't!" Her voice was suddenly fierce. "Don't kid me all the time. Don't!"

She got up and went to the window. She sat there on the window seat with her back to me, looking out across the East River. I crossed to her and for the second time put my hand on her shoulder. It was stiff, unwelcoming.

"I'm sorry."

"You laugh at me all the time. It isn't fair."

"I don't mean to."

"It isn't a joke, my writing. Some day I'll be good."

"I know you will."

She turned to me and put out her hand impulsively. "Oh, Peter, I'm such a pig. And you're so—so *good* to me. And *for* me," she added slowly. "It was only seeing your beautiful place, and the thought of it just being there all day, with nobody in it, nobody using it. If only" —and now the words came out in a rush—"if only I could use it for a few hours. I couldn't disturb anybody. I could let myself in and be gone long before you got home. . . ."

"Let yourself in?" I said slowly, and the reluctance in my voice took all the light out of her face. She sat down, drooping.

I thought of her as she had been earlier that evening, sitting right there where she was sitting now, looking up at me enraptured, by the beauty of the view, the apartment, the phonograph—everything. I felt a heel that I should have the place and hardly ever use it except to sleep, while she, with her determination to be a Great Writer, had to work jammed in a single room with another girl. I felt a heel for more reasons than that. I'd only invited her out because I'd got myself stuck with her. Now, I'd poked fun at her and she was young enough to be sensitive. I wanted to make amends. At least that's how I thought I was feeling.

I said, "Why don't you bring your work up here in the mornings? You're right, it wouldn't interfere with me. I'm always out by ten."

She swung around. "No," she said. "No."

"Why not?" I went to the desk and brought out a duplicate key. "Here. Let yourself in. I'll explain to the maid. She gets down every morning from Lottie's around ten-thirty or eleven."

She looked at the key as if it were a pigeon-blood ruby. Her hand went out to it, went back and then out again, taking it from me. Tears started to form in her eyes.

"I didn't think. . . . I never really dreamed. . . ."

"Forget it. Play the phonograph. Do anything you like to get in the mood."

She got up, still clutching the key. "I'll never be able . . ." The words choked up into a sob. She ran out of the apartment and closed the door behind her. I didn't follow to say goodnight.

I knew she didn't want me to see her crying.

CHAPTER FOUR

After she had left, I felt relaxed and contented as if I had been one hell of a generous guy. Soon I sat down at the desk and started my nightly letter to Iris. I had planned to tell her all about Nanny and the key but somehow it didn't come out right in words. Finally I made no mention of it at all.

Next morning at breakfast Lottie was silent and portentous. I suspected that Brian had told her about meeting Nanny and me outside the front door, and the fact that she didn't accuse me of moral depravity right there and then meant that she was taking it very heavily and was "waiting for the right moment." It was obvious that I would have to have things out with her soonor or later but I, too, decided to wait for the right moment. I slipped out into the kitchen and told Lucia, the daily woman, about Nanny. Lucia was fond of me and had Lottie's number. I gave her ten dollars, saying it would cover any extra work Nanny might cause and asked her not to mention it all to Lottie. She understood right away and grinned. I left for the office at quarter of ten. When I got back that evening, everything was neat as a nun but, propped up against the pile of Iris' letters from Jamaica on the desk by the window I found a little kid's drawing in ink. This time it was of a girl with hair tumbling over her face, sitting at a desk typing. Under it was typed:

Truman Capote thanks you;
Somerset Maugham thanks you;
I thank you.

The next day Miss Mills brought me a script that had come through the mail from an English professor in Ann Arbor. The moment I'd read it, I knew it was what I had been looking for. *Let Live* was its title. It was amusing and professional and inexpensive to produce with only one set and a cast of six. From then on, the office was geared up for an immediate production. I started working like a dog and coming home late. I never saw Nanny for a week or ten days, but every evening on my return there'd be a little picture. Once it was a girl listening to a phonograph with notes coming out of it; once it was a girl with two heads, one marked T. C., the other S. M.; once it was a girl bowed in despair ("Genius flagged today"); once it was just a great jagged flame with "burning, pure white" typed under it.

They always gave me a kick. They kept Nanny in my mind, but she was never in the apartment when I got home.

Lottie, inevitably, was wildly curious and enthusiastic about *Let Live* and had a field day with casting suggestions, ideas for sets and general interferences. In fact, it was all I could do to keep her from producing it, directing it, sticking together the costumes for it, and acting all the parts herself. She seemed to have forgotten about Nanny, and I forgot that I had decided to let her know what an innocent relationship it was.

One evening around six-thirty as I came home from the office, I ran into Lottie and Brian in the apartment house foyer. Without thinking, I invited them in for a drink. As I let them in the front door, I suddenly thought: Nanny! But it was all right. She had left.

There was a rather bad moment, however, when Lottie, always on the prowl, stopped at the desk and picked something up.

"Whatever is this meant to be?"

I took her a highball. She was studying Nanny's daily drawing. This time it was of a girl dancing with wild abandon. Under it was typed: *Triumphant Dance of Female Genius.*

I said, probably with a great deal too much nonchalance, "Oh, one of the stenographers from the office was here this afternoon doing the household checks. I guess she got carried away."

The gimlet gaze bored into me as Lottie dropped the drawing back on the desk.

"Well!" she said.

But she left it at that.

Iris wrote, excited and pleased that I had found a play. Her mother had completely convalesced and met a widow from California of whom she almost approved. With any luck, she said, she could leave her soon. I was enjoying myself. I always do in the first stages of a production.

And then, about a week later, I went home early from the office—around six. There was an opening and I had two tickets. I had been planning to take Alec Ryder, but he had flown to Chicago to check up on the touring company of one of his plays. When I let myself into the apartment, I heard the phonograph. I went into the living-room and there was Nanny sitting at the desk by the window, tapping away on a beat-up old typewriter that she must have brought with her.

When she saw me, she got up almost guiltily.

"Mercy, I lost all track of time. I'm sorry. I . . . ."

I was delighted to see her. "Hi," I said, "how about coming to the theater tonight? I have an extra seat."

She was worried about her clothes. She was wearing an old dirndl and a blouse with a scarlet chiffon scarf knotted at her throat. It was all wrong for an opening. That was the first time I realized she was about the same size as Iris. I went into the bedroom and picked out one of my wife's evening dresses. It was one she'd never liked very much, but I thought it would look good on Nanny. I gave it to her. She stayed in the bedroom quite a long time; then she called me in.

She was standing under the rather too splendid chandelier which Iris and I had fallen for one year in Italy and lugged home. In its sparkling illumination, Nanny was quite transformed. She'd fixed her face. It was the first time I'd seen her with make-up. The difference was remarkable. She still wasn't pretty, but she was intriguing-looking with that kind of suppressed sensuality which a lot of men go mad for. It wasn't the type of allure for me. But I was very aware of it, which was more than Nanny seemed to be. She acted as if there was no change in her appearance at all.

"It's been wonderful working here, I can't tell you."

"I'm glad."

"I've started my new story. From *Salomé*. 'The Secret of Love.'"

"Is it greater than the secret of death?"

"That's what it's meant to be about. I haven't been a nuisance, have I?"

"On the contrary, you've been a comfort."

"That's silly."

"No. Those drawings—they're a comfort to a busy, wifeless guy."

"Oh, I just feel like doing them. That's all. Did Charlotte Marin and her husband mind . . . I mean, about last time?"

"For heaven's sake, still harping on that! Of course not."

That night, for the first time, Bill, the night elevator man, looked at Nanny with interest and even winked at me.

We went to Sardi's for dinner because I figured her stomach wasn't used to the Theater habit of eating after the show. Then we went to the play. It wasn't much—one of those comedies about how a wise wife clings on to her intemperate husband against high odds. There was a party afterwards for the company but I didn't feel like going. Since Nanny had to change into her own clothes, we went back to the apartment.

Her working there had had an odd effect on me. Although I had never seen her at the desk until that night, the little drawings had made her somehow seem like family. Without asking, I made her a lemonade and fixed myself a drink. We sat down together on a couch, casual and intimate like people who live together.

For some reason it didn't seem to matter that I knew so little about her. She was just Nanny Ordway who lived in the Village with a girl friend, who thought business shouldn't take place in a pretty place, who had come to be a small part of my life. We had met by accident and drifted into a friendship by the accident of Iris' absence and mutual loneliness. It was one of those relationships that fall into no fixed category but happen all the time. There were no strings to it at all. Either of us could stop it tomorrow or it could go on indefinitely. That, I suppose, was what made it so pleasant.

We started to talk about the play and because of the play, about married love. Nanny thought the play was stupid. If a man loved his wife, he wouldn't run around with other women, and if he did run around with other women, he wouldn't go back and be in love with his wife all over again. She was very earnest about it. She was Nanny Ordway, the great twenty-year-old psychological author who knew the whole pitch on The Secret of Love.

She looked charming sitting there next to me in Iris' dress, like a kid sister of Iris' who had always been overshadowed. I felt fonder of her than I had ever been. Perhaps it was because I no longer had any qualms about my own motives. I had explained our relationship away to myself. I knew there wasn't the remotest chance of my falling in love with her or her with me.

"If you're in love, Peter, you're in love. If you stop being in love, you stop. You don't start again like a stalled motorboat."

"Why not?"

"Because you can't."

"You'd be surprised what people can do when they try."

"Peter, what nonsense!" she turned to me quickly. "You, for example, you could never possibly fall out of love with your wife and then in again. In again out again Finnegan."

"I couldn't?"

"Of course you couldn't. Nor she with you."

"But she did."

I didn't quite know why I'd made that admission. I never normally talked about Iris and myself with anyone. I suppose the atmosphere Nanny created was just right for it—the solemn, impersonal atmosphere of the very young who still think emotions are things to be analyzed.

Once I'd started, I went on. "A couple of years ago—in Mexico—Iris fell in love with another guy. Very much in love. It went wrong. It was all wrong from the beginning, I guess. But she fell in love with him. Then she fell back in love with me. The stalled motorboat. In again out again Finnegan."

Nanny looked horrified. "And all the time you went on being in love with her?"

"Sure."

"What was his name?"

"Iris' man? Martin. Why do you want to know?"

"Did you hate Martin?"

"No, not really."

"But it must all be there inside you. It was broken once. How could you ever get confidence back?"

"It isn't as hard as they say in the text books."

"But—but it can't be the same. Now you could fall out of love with her sometime."

"No."

"Not even if someone came along just as attractive and fascinating and amusing?"

I grinned. "Where would she come from? I've never met anyone one-tenth as attractive and fascinating and amusing as Iris."

She put down her lemonade glass. "Well," she said, "it could never be that way with me. Patched up, compromised. No—never." And then: "Isn't it funny?"

"What?"

"You and me—being friends when we're so different."

"It isn't funny."

"You'll forget me when your wife comes back."

"Of course I won't."

After I'd said that I realized it wasn't true. Once Iris was back, I'd probably forget Nanny Ordway in a week. Relationships between men and women were not as simple as I'd been pretending, I reflected. What did I really know about Nanny's feeling for me? Were these evenings valuable for her? Were they something she would miss? Maybe I had been a selfish, stupid male, using her unfeelingly as a salve for my temporary loneliness.

My insincerity had made me ashamed. Somehow or other, Nanny Ordway always ended up making me ashamed. I leaned over and kissed her on the cheek, feeling a little like Judas. It was the first time I'd kissed her. Her skin was dry, not very attractive.

"I won't forget you," I said. "Iris will want to know you too."

She got up quickly as if the kiss had been a wrong note. She glanced at her watch.

"Heavens, it's late. I'd better change back to my own dress."

She went into the bedroom and stayed there awhile. Then she came out in her old dirndl and blouse and her scarlet knotted scarf. She went to the desk and picked up her typewriter.

"Why not leave it there for tomorrow, Nanny?"

"Oh, no. I still have something to do tonight."

"That's the spirit. George Sand used to work until dawn."

She didn't smile. "Goodnight, Peter."

"I'll get you a taxi."

"No, no. Don't be silly. And don't come down. I'd rather really."

I took her to the elevator. With her typewriter and her old tweed coat, she looked like a shabby little stenographer. The elevator man cast her only a bored, sleepy glance. My feeling of guilt stirred again. I smiled and waved.

"Goodnight, Miss O'Dream. Do good work."

"Oh, I will. You can depend on that."

All next morning I worked at the office. The deal with

Thomas Wood, the author of *Let Live*, had been completed by now and I even had most of the production money lined up. I was reaching the casting stage and someone had recommended a minor Hollywood character actor for one of the big male roles. I had never seen him on the screen or if I had I had forgotten. I discovered he was playing in an old movie at one of the 42nd Street houses. After lunch, I went to take a look at his performance.

I liked him and thought he might do. I went back to the office around four o'clock to send a telegram to his agent in Hollywood. When I got there, Miss Mills brought me a cable from Iris. She was arriving at Idlewild at six o'clock that evening.

I was overjoyed. I made a couple of calls canceling business dates so that I could meet her at the airport. I was scared, if I called Lottie, that she would insist on coming with me and hogging the reunion scene, but I knew I'd never be forgiven if I kept her in the dark about The Great News. I compromised by having Miss Mills call her at the very last minute, explaining that I'd just got the cable and had had to rush right out.

The plane was ten minutes late. Many people suffer torments when someone they love is flying. But I was never that way about Iris. She was so real to me that the idea of anything destroying the reality was inconceivable. The plane appeared and landed. The moment I saw her coming down the gangplank, it was as if she had never been away.

When she came out of Customs, a couple of news photographers were hanging around. Because Iris had appeared in so many movies, she was really more of a celebrity than Lottie (although neither Lottie nor Iris would ever have dreamed of admitting it). Iris is shy with photographers. She's the most reluctant movie-star in history. But we kissed politely for the cameras, and after that they left us alone.

I got her into a taxi. She was looking wonderful, but then she always did. She had one of those faces, with large eyes and perfectly constructed bones, which nothing can damage. Sometimes I wished she was less beautiful, less doomed to be in the public domain. But that afternoon I felt only pride and contentment. I didn't even feel nervous the way you do in the early stages of love when separation may still have made a change and could demand re-adaptation.

She was in fine spirits, amusing about her mother and the white-mustached British colonel whom Iris had skilfully switched to mother. That was why she had felt she could leave her mother safely alone. She was interested about *Let Live*, and full of questions about Lottie.

"Is she still our best friend?"

"I'm afraid so. I've been having breakfast in bed with her and Brian every morning."

"Oh, dear, I was hoping you'd mortally offended her by now. Does she know I'm coming back?"

"It was as good as my life was worth. I had Miss Mills call. She'll be keening around the apartment like a banshee if I know Lottie. It's been tough for her with only Brian and me to supervise."

"Dear Lottie!"

"Alec Ryder's going to be pestering you to do that show in London."

"Don't worry. The Swan of Avon could come with a brand new Hamlet in his beak and there'd be no sale. I'm settling down for a year's run as a wife."

I hadn't really expected that Alec's offer would interest her, but that made my happiness complete. She started to fumble in her bag. She thought that women who were always asking men for cigarettes were bores. I lit one for her.

"Thank you, Peter. Well, how have you been?"

"Okay."

"You haven't been up to anything?"

"For heaven's sake, what makes you ask that?"

"I don't know. I always feel that when I've been away from you. I suppose it's smug and feminine. I like to think you need me."

"I need you."

She put her hand on my arm. "By the way, what happened to your girl genius? You stopped writing about her."

"Oh, Nanny Ordway? She's around."

"I'm dying to meet her."

Suddenly it occurred to me that Nanny Ordway might be in the apartment when we arrived home, still sitting at her typewriter with her dark hair floppily hiding her profile. When Iris' cable came, I'd never even thought of Nanny, let alone remembered to call and put her off. I felt absurdly uncomfortable. It didn't matter much. Iris wasn't sentimental about homecomings. But I had never explained to her about giving Nanny the key and, for some reason, it seemed hard to explain now. *"Oh, by the way, I let her work in the apartment. I meant to write you."*

Then I realized that it would be after seven by the time we got home. It had been six-thirty when I had taken Brian and Lottie in that day and Nanny hadn't been there. It seemed wiser to bank on the fact that she had left and then, later that evening, to explain the whole Nanny thing at length.

If I could explain it! Now Iris was back, I found that the exact nature of the relationship and its justification seemed to be eluding me.

"You'll see her soon," I said.

"Is she writing a play or something? Is that why you're interested in her?"

"Not exactly." I added with cowardice, "She's not very exciting."

Iris looked at me quickly. "Don't apologize, darling. I didn't want her to be exciting."

We'd crawled through the evening mid-town traffic and arrived at Sutton Place. The doorman and Bill, on the evening elevator shift, were pleased to see Iris. We reached our floor and I heard the phonograph playing inside. Bill carried Iris' suitcases to the door. I said:

"Okay. I'll take them in."

He went back to the elevator. Iris said, "Why's the phonograph playing? You don't suppose Lottie's putting on some frightful homecoming production?"

The phonograph was playing *Salomé*. I knew who was there and I felt very silly. I tried to be nonchalant bringing out my key.

"It's probably just Nanny."

"Nanny?" Iris looked blank. "Nanny Ordway?"

"I've been letting her write here while I'm at the office. She lives in a terrible dreary room in the Village. Maybe I'm a dope. I'll explain later."

I opened the door. For some reason Iris stood back and let me go in first.

Nanny's typewriter was on the desk by the window, but she wasn't in the living-room. The phonograph was going full blast. Salomé was screaming her lungs out over Jokanaan's severed head. Iris picked up a piece of paper that was propped on the desk against the pile of her letters from Jamaica.

"Whatever is this?"

Those damn drawings! I took it from her. This time it was a kid's circle and line sketch in ink of a girl hanging by the neck from a rope. Under it was typed in block capitals:

THE SECRET OF LOVE IS GREATER
THAN THE SECRET OF DEATH?

It was the sort of joke that had seemed cute with Nanny. Now it seemed extremely embarrassing. I dropped it back on the desk.

"It's just one of the fool drawings Nanny makes," I said.

"How very strange. Peter, would you mind turning down the phonograph. I feel as if John the Baptist's hair was in my mouth."

"Nanny's probably in the bathroom," I said.

I turned off the phonograph. Then I picked up Iris' suitcases and carried them toward the bedroom. The bathroom door was open and Nanny wasn't inside. Iris followed me into the bedroom. We both stopped on the threshold.

Nanny Ordway was there.

Her red chiffon scarf was knotted around her neck and she was dangling by it from the metal stem of the chandelier.

CHAPTER FIVE

She was twirling very slightly on the twisted scarf. Her hair had fallen forward screening her face like some ritual hood. A bedroom chair was lying kicked on its side beneath her dangling toes. Her heel had slipped out of one of the worn ballet shoes. There was a run in the stocking on her left leg.

I saw all the details in a moment of preternatural acuity, and I felt a kind of belated clairvoyance as if a voice were whispering inside me: "You see? This is what came of your harmless relationship."

I felt sick in the stomach but my mind was very clear. Close behind me, I heard Iris gasp.

I said, "Get Doctor Norris on the phone."

I put down the suitcases and ran to the kitchen. I found a carving knife in a drawer and ran back with it to the bedroom. I picked up the chair from under Nanny, climbed on it and cut the scarf loose from the chandelier. She fell the few feet to the ground with a thud like a sack. I should have supported her while I cut the rope. I hadn't thought of that.

I knelt down at her side. I tried to loosen the knot in the scarf at the nape of her neck but I couldn't free it with my fingers. Finally I frayed the scarf through with the knife.

I could hear Iris on the bedside phone. Dr. Norris was our physician and he lived in the next apartment house.

". . . yes, yes . . . come quickly. Please . . ."

Her voice sounded steadier than mine would have been. I looked down at Nanny Ordway. Her face was a dreadful purplish gray. There was a deep red furrow around her neck where the scarf had bit into the flesh. She wore the old dirndl and blouse, but she bore no resemblance to herself at all. She just looked like a corpse —any corpse.

But I couldn't be sure she was dead. I didn't know enough. Did you try artificial respiration when someone was hanged? I squatted there, trying to recapture what shreds of medical knowledge I possessed. But my mind wouldn't focus on that. All I was thinking was:

Nanny Ordway's committed suicide. Everyone's going to say she killed herself because of me.

Iris crossed to my side. "He's coming right away— Doctor Norris."

I looked up at her. I desperately needed some token to show that she was not going to condemn me. It was absurd to expect one, of course. How could she take a stand yet? She didn't know anything about it.

"He's coming," she said again.

There was something I should say quickly to allay the suspicions that must be forming in her mind. But I couldn't think of the right words. She must have guessed part of what I was feeling. She put her hand on my shoulder. My hand went up to cover hers. It was as if the floor between us had been splitting in an earthquake and she, somehow, with her hand on my shoulder, had miraculously managed to make it firm again.

There was a sharp rat-tat at the front door. We both ran to let in Dr. Norris. Lottie, with Brian behind her, exploded across the threshold. She was wearing an elaborate black cocktail dress dripping with pearls. She didn't seem quite real to me—like a figure out of some dim past.

"Iris, baby." Her arms, with a metallic clatter of bracelets, swooped around Iris' neck. "Welcome home, angel. Quick. Upstairs. Champagne before I go to the theater. And then dinner for you two with Brian. He's fixed it all. It's his party. It . . ."

She broke off, the gimlet gaze spreading from Iris' face to mine. "What's the matter? What's happened?"

I glanced instinctively back toward the bedroom.

"Get out, Lottie. Please get out."

"What is it?" She took a step into the room.

"Lottie!"

She pushed past me and hurried toward the bedroom. Neither Iris nor I moved. Then, in the bedroom, Lottie screamed. Brian dashed forward. Iris and I followed. Lottie was standing over Nanny Ordway. Her face was putty gray. She was twisting at the pearls around her throat, as if people actually did that outside of a play.

"It's the little girl! It's Peter's little girl!" She swung around to me. Her expression, her quick turn, the position of her hands all seemed inevitable. I might have rehearsed her in the scene time and time again. "How could you, Peter? How could you have done this to Iris?"

Brian put his hand on her arm. "Lay off, Lottie, for God's sake."

She pushed him contemptuously aside. She was Avenging Society, Outraged Womanhood, Betrayed Friend—everything merged into one. Of course she was. That's how I had expected Lottie to react. That was how everyone was going to react.

"Peter, she's killed herself! The poor little creature! You played around with her just because you were lonely. You turned her head. You . . ."

"Shut up, Lottie," said Iris.

A knock sounded again at the front door. I went back to answer it. Dr. Norris came hurrying in. He was a tall, tactful young man with an expensive suit and the assurance that comes from a large, fashionable practice.

He went with me into the bedroom. He looked down at Nanny and then at the rest of us.

"Yes," he said. "I think, if you please, you should all go into the other room."

We trooped back into the living-room. Dr. Norris shut the door on us. Iris' suitcases still stood by the threshold where I had dropped them. They were symbols of a homecoming. I expected Lottie to gesture at them flamboyantly. *Look! Poor Iris' suitcases! And she had to come home to this!* But she didn't. She was too busy, probably, checking with that trigger mind of hers. *He met her at my party. He took her out that first night. And then Brian told me how he caught them together in the hall. . . . A tawdry little affair. Plain as a pikestaff. To all intents and purposes—a murderer.*

In a few minutes, Dr. Norris put his head around the door. Coming through the crack, it looked disembodied —the head of a suave, clean-shaven John the Baptist who'd struck it rich with a Messianic cult in Southern California.

"I'm afraid she's dead. I recommend that one of you call the police immediately."

He said that with a kind of tactful lowness of voice as if he were recommending a sitz-bath. I suppose it wasn't much more important than that to him. The announcement wasn't very important to me, either. I'd already resigned myself to the fact of Nanny's death—suicide, police, everything.

But the news galvanized Lottie. Instantly she hurried toward the phone, eager to start things, to have the disaster go on. I couldn't dislike her for it. Why shouldn't she feel that way? A whacking great scandal—everybody's crazy about them.

Brian went after her. "Better let me do it, Lottie."

Lottie picked up the receiver. I crossed and took it from her. At least I had that much pride.

"Get me the police."

When I was connected, I said, "This is Peter Duluth." I gave the address. "You'd better send someone over right away. A girl's killed herself."

My voice sounded all right, but when I dropped the receiver back onto the stand, my hand was shaking. I crossed to the bar.

Lottie cried, "Iris, stop him. He mustn't drink. Not now."

The absurdity, the typical Lottiness of that remark, made everything a little less awful, somehow. Comedy always helps, I suppose. It also helped that Iris went straight to the bar and mixed me a Scotch and water. She mixed one for herself and one for Brian too.

"Lottie," she said, "it's after seven-thirty. You've got to go to the theater."

"The theater. My God, the theater!" Lottie had plunged into one of her "My God" routines. "How can I? How can I go to the theater?"

"Troopers," I said. "They go bravely on with the show, hissing through stiff upper lips, remember?"

She swung around to me. "But, Peter, how can I leave you in this ghastly situation? How can I do it?" I wasn't the pariah any more. Suddenly I had become the Best Friend in Distress, the to-be-supported . . . championed . . . protected-one. She clutched me and kissed me with extravagant affection. "Darling, you mustn't worry. Promise me not to worry. I won't say a word to the police. You can depend on that. Oh, God, how could you have done it? How could you have let this happen? I warned you. Didn't I warn you? A little girl, a mere child . . ."

"Lottie dear," said Iris, "please go."

"Oh, I'm going." Of course she was going. She was beginning to realize how she could knock them all dead at the theater with the great news. I wasn't anxious about her performance, either. She had the sensitivity of a rhinoceros. "Peter, darling, don't worry about the play. I'll manage somehow. And don't do anything foolish with the police. Leave it all to me. I'll be back right after the show. Oh, my dears, my poor darlings!"

She started in a hawklike swoop for the door. Brian gulped down his drink.

"I'd better see she gets there okay." He looked pale and shaken but he patted my arm. "That's my boy, Peter. I'll come right back from the theater. If you want me, I'll be upstairs."

He followed Lottie out of the apartment and closed the door. I had been dreading the moment when I'd be alone with Iris. Not because I was afraid she'd judge me. She wasn't a bit like Lottie. She didn't jump before she knew. And she was my wife, which was as important to her as to me. But, so long as Lottie had been there making a fool of herself, the time for explaining had been postponed. Now, I would have to explain. And how could I—when I couldn't understand it myself, when all that I felt was bafflement and panic and an obscure guilt-sense which nagged that I deserved whatever punishment was coming to me.

I tried to remember Nanny Ordway, how she had looked, how it had been like with her, what our encounter had really amounted to, but all that came up in my mind was that purple-faced corpse in the next room.

Iris lit a cigarette. She hadn't looked tired when she

got off the plane. But now she did—tired and almost her age, which was thirty-four. Seeing her suffer and knowing it was my doing made me suddenly, unreasonably angry.

"Okay, she's dead," I said. "She's killed herself. There it is. We're stuck with it. Lottie thinks it's my fault. The police will say it's my fault. To hell with it—who cares?"

Iris looked at me. "Peter, don't be stupid. Who do you think you're talking to? Just tell me the truth."

"The truth? I saw her a couple of times. I thought she was a nice enough kid. She amused me. She was someone to be with. I guess I was sorry for her. I gave her the key. I let her bring her work here. Okay. I suppose I was going paternal and senile in my old age. But there it is. That was the set-up. Now she's killed herself. Who's going to believe me? The blue-bottomed baboon with the lowest intelligence quota at the Bronx Zoo?"

Iris came to me, still holding her glass. "I'll believe you."

Saying that so quickly and simply, she took me off my guard. My anger fizzled out. Without it, I felt rudderless. "You . . . you . . ."

"You wouldn't lie to me." She paused. "But she fell in love with you?"

Suddenly I found I didn't have to be affected about it. I could talk naturally. That was what she'd done for me.

"My God, I don't think so. She never showed the slightest sign. Why should she have fallen in love with me? It wasn't ever on that level. She made a fetish of friendship. We were friends. She kept on saying it. Friends. Besides, from the beginning she knew all about you, that I was in love with you. We were always talking about you."

"Which doesn't prevent a twenty-year-old girl falling in love, does it?"

"But she didn't. You've got to take my word for it. Baby, I'm not Peter Pan. I've had women in love with me before. I can't have been that much of a fool."

"You didn't even kiss her?"

"Yes. I kissed her—once, because . . . Hell, I can't remember why. But it wasn't anything."

"It wasn't? Not for a young impressionable girl who . . ."

I put my hand on her arm. "Baby, can't you tell? Isn't there some way? Can't you see, feel that there's nothing changed, that I love you, that I couldn't be making things up?"

Her dark, steady eyes watched me. "I believe you. And if you say so, I believe she wasn't in love with you either." She crossed to the desk and picked up Nanny's sketch of the hanging girl. I could tell she was making a great effort to be calm—to help me. "And this?"

"She always made little drawings. I told you. It was a kind of running gag. When I saw it, I thought it just meant that her writing hadn't been going well today. I . . ."

" 'The secret of love is greater than the secret of death.' "

"Okay. I know what it sounds like, but it's a quote from *Salomé*. She was using it for the title of a story. That was a kind of running gag too. We seemed to go in for gags, didn't we? Laugh? Never laughed so much in our lives!"

Iris dropped the drawing and leafed through a pile of manuscript pages which Nanny must have left.

"What about her parents? We'll have to phone them or something, won't we?"

"I don't know anything about them. I just know that she lived in the Village with another girl."

Iris turned from the desk. Very quietly, she said, "I don't think the police are going to believe all this, do you?"

"No."

"Then we'll just have to hope for the best."

She crossed back to me. I put my arms around her. But I didn't dare kiss her. I was afraid, if I did, I might break down and cry like a child.

CHAPTER SIX

Dr. Norris emerged from the bedroom then. He was wearing a subdued version of his crisp, everything's-going-to-be-all-right smile. Under the circumstances it was ludicrous.

"Well, Peter, you called the police?"

"Yes."

"Fine. I'm afraid she'd been dead for some time. No chance to have saved her. Most unfortunate for you both. No close friend, I hope?"

"No."

"Some disappointed actress, perhaps, poor kid."

Dr. Norris was an amateur enthusiast of the stage and read all those stories about how heartbreaking it is to get established in the Theater. I don't know why he imagined that disappointed actresses committed suicide in the bedrooms of producers. Maybe he had only said it to be tactful, to minimize the degree of my responsibility.

Iris said, "I suppose there are no complications?"

"About the suicide? The pressure marks of the ligature seem a little atypical. But that's hardly my line. Let's leave that to the police, shall we?"

I didn't know what that meant, but it sounded ominous. Dr. Norris glanced at the gold watch on his neat wrist.

"If you'll excuse me, I should call the wife. A cocktail party we were going to."

I would have to get used to the fact that my tragedy

was only a minor inconvenience to other people. I heard him being discreet and impersonal on the phone.

"I'm sorry, dear . . . shall be detained . . . yes, of course, go alone if you like . . . explain to Madge and Billy . . ."

He replaced the phone, came over and sat with us while we waited for the police, polite and noncommittal, treating us delicately, like a surgeon handling a diseased appendix. He didn't ask any questions. That wasn't his business. He had to be professional at all costs. I'd never realized before that I didn't like him.

In about ten minutes, the police arrived—four of them, three plainclothes detectives and a police officer. The chief of the detectives was tall and young with a very soft voice. He and the officer went almost immediately into the bedroom with Doctor Norris. The other two detectives started to prowl around the living-room. Iris showed one of them Nanny's drawing. He took it, Nanny's manuscript and Nanny's typewriter, retreating with them into the bedroom. Soon I was called after him. I had to describe how Nanny had been hanging, how the scarf had been before I cut it. Then I was sent back to the living-room.

Another man was arriving, big and red-faced, with a black bag. I could tell he was an assistant medical examiner for the M. E.'s office. I'd been to the movies. I'd read books. I knew the things that had to happen. But they didn't seem convincing in my own apartment. I hadn't taken a second drink, but the shock and the first drink had managed now to give everything a patina of unreality and a kind of cynical humor—as if the whole thing was a terribly sour joke against myself.

And against Iris, of course—that's what made it so very sour.

In a few minutes, the young, tall detective came out of the bedroom. He looked about thirty-five and he moved very quietly, giving an impression of calm. It wasn't the laboriously rehearsed calm of Dr. Norris; it seemed natural to him, as if he'd given up being surprised by anything years ago. He was good-looking, with a certain ascetic quality to his unobtrusive features and gray eyes. He reminded me of a Jesuit priest who was a friend of mine—the cleverest man I knew.

I wondered if it was going to make it better or worse that he was obviously not a straight tough cop. I wondered, too, whether it was he who was going to be my antagonist. Perhaps he was just a subsidiary character slipping in and out. Maybe the Real Enemy would come later.

For I had resigned myself to the fact that the police would be The Enemy. I knew what my story sounded like. I knew where they were going to lay the moral blame.

He came to us as if he were meeting us at a cocktail party. "My name is Trant—Lieutenant Trant of the Homicide Bureau. You're Mr. Duluth, a producer and director in the Theater." His gaze, unsmiling but not hostile, shifted to Iris. "I've seen you, Mrs. Duluth, in the movies and on the stage. Often."

He ignored the two other detectives who were still milling around. He glanced at a chair, waiting for Iris' permission to sit. She nodded. He drew the chair up close to us and sat down. I thought: It's going to be worse with him than with a regular cop—much worse.

He said, "Just a few questions. First, the girl's name?"

"Nanny Ordway," I said.

"Nanny Ordway. She was living here with you?"

"No. She lives at 31 Charlton Street in the Village."

He took out an old envelope, scribbled the name and address on its back, and returned it to his pocket.

"Who discovered her?"

"We both did. My wife's just back from Jamaica. I'd

been to the airport to meet her. When we got here just after seven, we found her."

"I see. And how did she happen to be in your apartment?"

"She had a key. She came every day—to write."

"Something for you—a play?"

"No. Just writing. She was only beginning. Hadn't had anything published."

"I see." He said that again in his quiet, pleasant, unassuming voice. "And why did she have a key and do her writing here, Mr. Duluth?"

"I gave her the key. She was living down there in the Village with another girl. The conditions weren't any too good for writing. This place was empty all day. It was more convenient for her to come here."

It was sounding even weaker than I had expected. I could hear it all through Lieutenant Trant's ears, the way you can hear something you've written objectively by reading it to someone else. I was still hoping, though, that he was intelligent enough to accept it at its face value—because, after all, it was true.

He said, "When did you give Miss Ordway the key, Mr. Duluth?"

"About a week, ten days ago."

"You have known her a long time?"

"Just about four or five weeks."

Iris put in, "He met her the day I left for Jamaica. He wrote me about it."

Lieutenant Trant's courteous gaze shifted to her and then came back to me. I was so attuned to him by then that I could read his thoughts. He was already thinking: So. This is one of those set-ups where the noble wife sticks by the erring husband. He was missing the point. I felt angry as if he had insulted Iris out loud. It was a help to feel angry with him. It put me on the offensive.

"Where did you meet her, Mr. Duluth?"

"Upstairs at a party at Charlotte Marin's."

"Charlotte Marin, the actress?"

"That's right. She and her husband live in the apartment above. They asked me up to a party—the day my wife left for Jamaica. I met Nanny Ordway there."

"She was a friend of Charlotte Marin and her husband?"

"No. Some other people had brought her to the party. They didn't know her."

"What people?"

"I don't know."

The other detectives were taking fingerprints from the desk. They acted as if we weren't there, utterly indifferent to our quiet colloquy. It was like talking late at night in an office with scrubwomen sweeping around you.

Lieutenant Trant said, "And after you'd met her, you saw a great deal of her?"

"No. That night I took her out to Hamburger Heaven because she was hungry. I walked her to the subway. After that, I had dinner once at her place. She came once to the office. I took her to dinner once—no, twice. Those were the only times I saw her."

"I see." Lieutenant Trant watched me. "Are you in the habit of giving keys to young girls whom you hardly know?"

He hadn't said that as a taunt. He had asked it quietly as a question to which the answer might be mildly interesting. But its implications were plain. He'd summed me up as a routine Park Avenue libertine with an itch for change and a complaisant wife. He was too intelligent to be running around pigeon-holing people that quickly. He was being a lousy detective. My anger broke through the surface.

"For God's sake, you don't have to be clever and try to trip me up. If there'd been anything physical or romantic between Nanny Ordway and myself, I'd have told you. Why not? It isn't a criminal offense to have slept with a girl who killed herself. Everyone's going to believe I did, anyway. It's going to be yelled out by the newspapers tomorrow. What have I got to win by lying? There was nothing between Nanny Ordway and me. I was trying to be kind to her. It didn't work. That's all. I'm only interested in telling you the truth because finding the truth is supposed to be your job. And I'm damned if I'll have motives attributed to me that don't exist."

"And while we're on the subject, Lieutenant," put in Iris, "you might as well know that my husband and I are not giddy members of the International Set. We don't run around having affairs with all and sundry. We happen to be an ordinary, fairly solid married couple who love each other."

I felt a warm rush of gratitude to Iris, but Lieutenant Trant's only reaction was a sudden, rather mechanical smile. I don't think he was liking either of us any more. But he couldn't have been more unruffled—or more unimpressed.

"I'm glad to hear that you are both citizens in good standing. And I'm glad to hear your point of view toward truth, Mr. Duluth. I will bear it in mind."

He took a manila envelope from his pocket. Out of it, holding it by one corner, he brought Nanny Ordway's last sketch.

"You've seen this?"

"I have."

"Does it seem to you to be a suicide note?"

"I don't know what it seems to me to be. She always left me a note every day with a drawing on it, and some kind of a crack."

"You have the other notes?"

I tried to remember. "No. I don't think so. I think I always tore them up." I thought of the first note of all—the girl sitting at the telephone with the phone number floating above. I had taken it to the office. I had put it in my wallet. I took out my wallet. The drawing was there. I handed it to Lieutenant Trant.

"This is the first one. I kept it for the phone number."

"The phone number?" Lieutenant Trant took it and put it down on his knee. He glanced at it and then back to the other one in his hand.

"A hanging girl. The secret of love is greater than the secret of death. A query has been added after the word 'death.' Doesn't that suggest suicide, Mr. Duluth?"

" 'The secret of love'—that's a quote from *Salomé*. She was writing a story with that as its theme."

"Nevertheless, doesn't it suggest suicide?"

"I don't know what it suggests."

"The secret of love—the secret of death. If it does suggest suicide—doesn't it also suggest that there was more than nothing between you?"

"It may look like that to you, but I swear . . ."

"There's no need to swear, Mr. Duluth. We know you are telling the truth. You've made that plain. Can you suggest any motive for suicide other than an unsuccessful affair with a married man?"

"I hardly knew her. I told you that. There was her writing. Maybe she was discouraged about her writing. Don't writers get discouraged about writing?"

"But she's dead in *your* apartment, Mr. Duluth. If she'd had some motive for committing suicide which did not concern you, would she have embarrassed you by using your apartment to hang herself in? Or are the conditions in the Village as little convenient for hanging as for writing?"

I looked back at him, wondering dimly where he

59

came from. This wasn't at all type-casting for a police detective. His face was quite secular and modern really, but I couldn't escape that medieval priestly impression. A young Inquisitor, maybe? I thought, dimly too, about Truth. I knew the truth. He was trying to get to the truth. All he had to do was to believe me, but I could talk till I was blue in the face and he wouldn't be convinced. I didn't envy anyone whose job was to find the Truth.

Maybe, if Nanny Ordway had never existed, I would have liked Lieutenant Trant.

"Mr. Duluth, did Miss Ordway seem to you like a neurotic girl?"

"No more than anyone else."

"Quite normal?"

"That's how she seemed to me."

I got the straight gray gaze then. Yes, it was an Inquisitor. He had a fanaticism about something—justice, possibly, or the protection of young girls from vile seducers?

"Then you're not surprised that I should be interested in discovering why a normal young girl committed suicide in your apartment?"

"I'm not surprised at all."

"But the whole thing is a complete mystery to you?"

"A complete mystery."

Dr. Norris came out of the bedroom then. He gave me his cold cheerful smile as he hurried toward the door.

"So long, Peter. If there's anything the wife or I can do—just give us a buzz." He waved at Iris. "Goodnight. Good luck."

I felt frustrated and ferocious. I wanted to vent it on someone. I called after him. "Give my love to Madge and Billy at the cocktail party."

He turned. "I didn't know you knew them, Peter. I . . . oh, yes."

He scuttled out of the door like the White Rabbit. *"Oh, dear, oh, dear, I shall be late."*

Lieutenant Trant got up and went back to the bedroom. Two white-coated attendants with a stretcher came in the front door and disappeared into the bedroom too. The apartment didn't seem ours any more. It had lost all identity. It was impersonal as the Morgue.

I lit a cigarette. Iris smiled at me. It was meant to be a reassuring smile.

"At least you let him have it."

"For all the good it did."

Soon Lieutenant Trant came out of the bedroom again. This time he didn't sit down. His manner was obscurely more official.

"Mr. Duluth, I wondered if you'd tell me where you were this afternoon."

"I left the office about five to go to the airport."

"And before that?"

"I went to a movie."

"A movie?"

"I'm casting a play. There's a Hollywood actor I'm interested in. He was playing in a movie in one of those 42nd Street houses. I went there to see him."

"Which movie house?"

"I didn't notice which one, but it's easy to find out."

"What was this movie?"

"Happy Ending. That was its improbable title."

"You went alone?"

"That's right—alone."

Lieutenant Trant was shifting his balance from one foot to the other. "I suppose you won't object to coming around to the station-house to make a statement?"

"Of course not."

Iris got up. "I'll come too."

Every now and then reality broke through to me. I turned to her, remembering that she had just come off a plane, that it was after nine, that she hadn't eaten anything, that she hadn't even washed up or opened her suitcases.

"Baby, don't come. Please. You'll knock yourself out."

"You don't have to come, Mrs. Duluth," said Lieutenant Trant. "You can make a brief corroborative statement of the discovery here."

"Of course I'm coming. There's no regulation against it, is there, Lieutenant?"

"I'm afraid you can't sit in on your husband's statement." Lieutenant Trant smiled at her. Maybe it was my overworked imagination, but it seemed to me a pitying smile. "But you can come to the station-house if you want to. And, if you're hungry, the boys can bring you in something to eat. You'll find a lot of fans down there."

Fans! That was going to make it even worse, of course. Iris was a celebrity. That was going to dog us all the way through.

She picked up the coat she had dropped in a chair by the door when we came in from the airport. She slung it over her shoulders. "Do you mind if I ask you one thing, Lieutenant?"

"Of course not. Go ahead."

Iris started putting on her gloves, working the leather down over each finger methodically, not the way she ever did it in real life but the way directors go in for in the movies.

"Why do you want to know where my husband was this afternoon? What difference does it make?"

"I'm afraid we're nosy, Mrs. Duluth."

"But if it's suicide . . ." She paused and added very quietly. "It is suicide, isn't it, Lieutenant?"

Lieutenant Trant's answering voice was just as quiet and just as casual. "Oh, I expect so, Mrs. Duluth. The M.E.'s office will have to decide that. It's much too early to be sure yet. The pressure marks around the neck look normal enough, but both the assistant M.E. and Dr. Norris noticed certain discrepancies. But I imagine the boys up at Bellevue will be able to figure out a satisfactory explanation. Meanwhile, however . . ."

He broke off. He looked suddenly tired as if he was disgusted with us, disgusted with Nanny Ordway, disgusted with everything that made life complicated.

"We always keep an open mind until we're sure, Mrs. Duluth. An open mind. Suicide . . . murder . . ."

CHAPTER SEVEN

We drove with Lieutenant Trant to the station-house. I'd never been there before and I hadn't realized it was so near. It was hard to grasp the fact that all the time we had been living with reasonable peacefulness in our apartment, other people's difficulties, sufferings, trage-dies had been reaching some sort of climax only a stone's throw away. A sorting house for anger, frayed nerves, and despair—and I had passed it indifferently almost every day.

We went into a reception office where a sergeant was seated behind a high desk and a few vague people waited on wooden benches. We climbed some stairs to the Detectives' Room. It was large, high-ceilinged, and bleak with rusty white walls and geometrically spaced desks. There was an austere, barrackish atmosphere which re-minded me of navy boot-camp. Four or five detectives were lounging around with the bored indolence of a slack period. A radio was playing a commercial.

Lieutenant Trant took us over to a young man sitting at a desk in a corner.

"Jim, take a statement from Mrs. Duluth. Discovery of body, presumed suicide."

The young man's eyes widened as he looked at Iris. "Gee, Iris Duluth."

"That's right. Go get her something to eat if she wants it. She's going to wait for her husband." He smiled again at Iris. "When you're through—maybe she'll give you her autograph."

He beckoned to another detective. We left Iris at the desk and the three of us went into an office. It was hardly a real office, just a compartment cut off the squad room with beaver-board partitions. Somehow I had expected something more impressive for Lieutenant Trant, but as he took the wooden swivel chair behind the neat desk, I saw it was the right set for him—the ascetic in his cell.

The detective had a short-hand machine. He was sitting unobtrusively by the door. Lieutenant Trant glanced at him.

"All right, Mr. Duluth. Now the statement. I won't interrupt you. First a simple statement covering the discovery of the body. Then a second statement giving in detail the whole history of your relationship with Miss Ordway. Mention any people and their addresses who can corroborate it." He paused, watching me with that polite gaze which wasn't actually hostile but suggested hostility. "Needless to say, you're not under arrest. There's nothing to arrest you for and there's no reason in the world why you should give the second statement at the present time if you don't want to."

"I want to."

I gave both statements. I no longer bothered about how it all sounded. I just detailed everything which had happened between Nanny Ordway and myself as accurately as I could.

To begin with, I found the clicking of the short-hand machine discomforting. But soon I forgot it. There was a sort of anesthetic quality about that gaunt little office— or rather, an insulating quality. I could hear the radio in the squad room. I could even hear snatches of voices, including Iris' voice. But I seemed shut off from the rest of life. I didn't think about being tired or afraid or angry. I didn't even worry much about what was going to happen in the future. I just gave the statement. Already it seemed stale and meaningless, like a playscript I'd been doctoring for weeks and was all set to abandon. Nanny Ordway, Nanny Ordway, Nanny Ordway . . . The only corroborative witnesses I could think of were Lottie and Brian, Miss Mills who had seen Nanny once at the office, and Lucia, the maid, who presumably had been seeing her every day working in the apartment. I knew Miss Mills' address, and I happened to have Lucia's in my pocket address-book. The whole thing took about an hour.

When I had finished, Lieutenant Trant dismissed the detective. "Start getting them typed up, Sam. Mr. Duluth can read them through and sign them tomorrow."

The detective went away. Lieutenant Trant and I continued to sit face to face. It had all seemed deceptively tranquil. Surely, I thought, there should have been some sort of bustle—telephone calls, policemen reporting. I was coming out of the ether a bit. It would have been easier if things had been going on. At least, it would have given a feeling of stature as if I were implicated in something that had some importance to someone.

I said, "Well—what now?"

Surprisingly Lieutenant Trant smiled. It was quite a wonderful face when he smiled. He could have been on the movies. Only on the movies he wouldn't have been playing a cop. He'd have been a doctor, maybe, or a young scientist dedicated to the pursuit of some noble end.

"There's nothing now, Mr. Duluth. Nothing—at present. I'd like you to come in tomorrow at ten. We may know a little more then."

I looked at him, trying to gauge what impression my full-length statement had had on him. He wasn't revealing anything.

I said, "Just exactly what is my status?"

"Your status? At the moment, Mr. Duluth, your status with the police is virtually nothing, too. You are just a man implicated in the suicide of a girl and, as you pointed out yourself, it is not a criminal offense to have been acquainted with a suicide. Once the M.E.'s office has established the fact of suicide, you will merely be a witness. On the other hand, of course, if the M.E.'s office is not satisfied with the evidence . . ."

He let the sentence drop there. His smile was exasperating now. I think he meant it to be.

I said, "Why do you keep on hinting that it may not be suicide?"

"As I told your wife, we have to keep our minds open. In any case, the idea that she might not have killed herself was originated by you."

"By me?"

"Over and over again you have denied the fact that Miss Ordway had any reason to kill herself because of you. There's usually a motive for suicide. And if there is no motive . . ."

He broke off again. I felt tired and intimidated by his unflagging, hopelessly misguided cleverness.

"You're smart, aren't you?" I said.

He shrugged. "If I was smart I'd be out making a fortune producing plays on Broadway. I wouldn't be a homicide detective."

"Why are you one anyway?" I was interested.

"That's a long story, Mr. Duluth, of very little concern to anyone but myself." He got up and held out his hand. "You'd better go rescue your wife from her fans. Tomorrow? At ten?"

I took his hand. I realized that the possibility of murder had to be considered at this stage. I knew that it would soon evaporate. But I also knew that, if Lieutenant Trant ever thought I was guilty of any crime punishable by law, he would track me to the ends of the earth. It was a peculiar sensation shaking his hand.

I said, "I'd hate to be your mouse, Lieutenant."

"My mouse?" He took his hand away. "Oh, I don't suppose you will be, Mr. Duluth. Goodnight."

I walked out into the squad-room. Iris was sitting at one of the desks with a paper coffee cup in her hand. A couple of detectives were standing around her—and three other men. When they saw me, the three men hurried toward me. Iris got up, looking at me anxiously. I knew what the men were, of course, and I was as ready as I would ever be for them. The second phase was beginning, the phase that didn't involve the police but would probably be worse.

I didn't know any of the reporters. They must have been legmen who'd dropped into the station-house on a routine check-up. They bombarded me with questions.

"Was she an actress?"

"No."

"A personal friend—a close personal friend?"

"Just a girl." I pushed past them to Iris. I was feeling dead beat now.

"How'd she come to be strung up in your bedroom? Mr. Duluth, give us a break, will you?"

"Skip it. For God's sake, skip it. You can get it all from the cops anyway."

I took Iris' arm and hurried down the stairs and out past the sergeant at the night desk. The reporters started to follow; then they gave up. But they'd left their feeling with me—that feeling of exposure. I was going to be a seven-day's wonder. Of course I was. It had everything as a moron's news story—movie-star wife, theatrical producer, young girl dead, sex . . .

I felt old and disgusted and unclean.

We didn't take a taxi. There wasn't any point. We

only lived around the corner. It was still quite early. People were passing us on the monotonous cross-town street, going about their ordinary evening affairs.

Iris put her arm through mine.

I said, "Did you get anything to eat, baby?"

"Just a cup of coffee. I wasn't hungry."

"The reporters bother you?"

"Just about what you'd expect."

"It'll be slapped over the headlines tomorrow."

"Yes." She glanced at me. "How did the statement go?"

"Okay, I guess."

"How was Lieutenant Trant?"

"Quiet and polite and professionally sinister."

"I don't like him," said Iris.

Did I? I didn't know. But there was going to be plenty of time for me to make up my mind whether I liked Lieutenant Trant or not.

We reached our apartment house. It was about eleven-thirty. The night porter knew; the night elevator man knew, too. Neither of them said anything, but you could tell. There was a whole new feeling. I was a goldfish in a bowl. They were peering in through the glass.

I opened the apartment door with my key. God knows, I never wanted to set foot in the place again, but that's what people have to do. You have a lease. You don't just walk out because a girl hung herself from your chandelier.

The lights were all on in the living-room. There weren't any visible policemen. I heard someone in the bedroom, though. Then Miss Mills emerged into the living-room.

Miss Mills was no beauty. She was plump and rather pig-faced and she wore a pair of rimless pince-nez on a gold chain which emphasized the snout-effect of her nose. But it never occurred to you to want her changed. That was the way Miss Mills always had been and always would be.

She came to us with her usual, integrated smile. She was the most comforting thing I'd seen that evening.

"Hello. I was in the box-office tonight and dear Lottie told me the news. I came right around. There was right smart of cops messing about, but I talked them into letting me stay. They've just left, thank God, and I've straightened up a bit."

She kissed Iris. "You must be beat from the plane and everything. You're both coming to my place to sleep. There's no point in spending a Charles Addams night here, and Lottie would grab you for upstairs anyway, which is a fate worse than et cetera."

I don't know how Miss Mills always seemed able to strike the right note in the least likely manner.

"I've packed an overnight thing for you, Peter. Iris' bags hadn't been unpacked. Thank God for small mercies. Stinking little bitch, hanging herself in your apartment. Shall we go right away? Or have a drink first? A drink, maybe?"

The phone rang. She went to answer it. "Sorry, no comment." She slammed down the receiver. "Goddam newspapermen. That's the fifteenth time."

She crossed to the bar and started mixing drinks, the pince-nez wabbling on the end of her nose. The atmosphere was warm and relaxed. It was phony, of course, but she'd managed to make us feel everything was all right.

Before she'd finished mixing the drinks, the phone rang again. She took the receiver off the stand and threw it down on the table.

"Here."

She brought us our drinks. Miss Mills would be

wonderful on a sinking ship, I thought. She'd have the orchestra playing, false noses handed around, and sandwiches sent up from the kitchen.

The door buzzer rang. Miss Mills went to answer it. Lottie burst in. She was still wearing the black dress and the pearls. She looked like a cocktail guest absurdly late for a party.

"Darlings . . ." She saw Miss Mills and broke off. Lottie didn't like Miss Mills. She thought she was too possessive of Iris and me and she also thought of her as an "underling."

"What are *you* doing here?"

"Helping," said Miss Mills.

"Well!" Brushing past her, Lottie hurried toward Iris and me, her arms outstretched. "My poor darlings. Where are the police?"

"They've gone," I said.

"Already?" She looked disappointed. But only for a moment. There was enough excitement without the police. She reached me and kissed me, smiling a smile of infinite tenderness. "Peter, darling, you should have been at the theater tonight. You really should. It would have warmed your heart to know what real friends you have. All of them—everyone of them in the cast—agreed with me. It's terrible for you. Shocking. That dreadful, twisted little girl doing this ghastly thing to you. So inconsiderate. Such a martyrdom. All of them, Peter, all those people, who hadn't even known her the way I had, agreed. They're sure there was nothing between you, that you did nothing you could blame yourself for. Just terrible, terrible bad luck. They're all with you, Peter, all with you one hundred per cent. Hello, Iris."

She kissed Iris perfunctorily. At the moment Iris was the less interesting of the two of us.

"Peter, you really should have been there. Phyllis

Hatcher almost passed out. And the old man—the one who plays the porter in the last act—never can remember his name—he was terribly broken up. And Gordon Ling dried up twice in the first act. Oh, but we got through it all right. Don't worry. Jammed house. Wonderful audience. And now . . ."

She swooped to the phone. "Why have you got the receiver off?" She picked it up and started to dial.

"Who are you calling, Lottie?" I asked.

"Brian, of course. To see if he's got the beds ready for you. You don't imagine I'd let you sleep here."

"We're going to Miss Mills', Lottie."

"What? . . . Hello, Brian, dear . . . *What* did you say, Peter?"

"We're sleeping at Miss Mills'."

Lottie glared from above the receiver. "But that's ridiculous. Of course you're spending the night with us."

"Sorry, Lottie, but it's all arranged."

"But you can't. Miss Mills' tiny flat? There isn't enough room for a stray cat. . . . What, Brian?" She'd picked up a pencil and was making her angry doodles all over the back of a playscript. "No, hold on a minute." She put her hand over the mouthpiece. "Peter—Iris."

"I'm sorry, Lottie dear," said Iris, "but it was all arranged before you came."

"Well, really!" Lottie's hand came off the mouthpiece. "No, Brian, never mind. It's all right. Never mind. I'll be up in a minute."

She slammed down the receiver. The phone started to ring. She picked the receiver up again.

"Yes? Oh, yes, of course, just a minute." She cupped the mouthpiece again. "Peter, it's the *News*."

"Tell them I'm not here."

"Mr. Duluth isn't here." Lottie put down the phone

again. "Really, this going to Miss Mills' is all too absolutely preposterous."

Miss Mills had picked up one of Iris' suitcases and my overnight bag. She was standing by the door.

"Come on," she said. "Let's go before she carries you bodily upstairs like Medea and her two dead infants."

Miss Mills' apartment on East 64th Street was small, but its very smallness and spinsterish chintzy quality encouraged a mood of cosiness and safety. Miss Mills scrambled some eggs and made us eat them with glasses of milk. Then she sent us to bed. She'd made up a bed for herself on the studio couch in the living-room. Iris and I had the bedroom.

We undressed and got together into Miss Mills' bed. I took my wife in my arms. The warmth and comfort of her was something I had almost forgotten, something to which, obscurely, I felt I had no right. I felt shy with her and very unhappy.

I said because I had to, "You do believe me, don't you?"

"Yes, Peter, I believe you."

"If there had been anything between Nanny and . . ."

"Don't talk about it, darling. There's no need."

Her head was on my shoulder. Her hair was soft against my cheek. It was almost all right. But part of my mind was still grinding on, obsessed by Nanny Ordway. Could she, after all, have been in love with me? Could she fantastically have misconstrued everything I had said and done—my telephone calls, my invitations to dinner, the giving of the key? Had all her talk about friendship been just a front? Could I have been that clumsy and blind?

Tomorrow there would be Lieutenant Trant again. Tomorrow there would be the newspapers. Would it all make any difference with *Let Live?* Would any of the backers take out their money? Maybe reporters had called the apartment after we'd left and Lottie had gabbed some of her bushwah to them. Iris would have to write to her mother in Jamaica. Her mother would send back a blast. Probably she would advise Iris to leave me. Probably . . .

My wife's hand slid down my thigh and slipped into my hand.

"Peter, stop thinking."

"But, baby . . ."

"It's all right. I love you and I believe you. It's all right, Peter. Go to sleep."

But she was as wide awake as I.

CHAPTER EIGHT

When Iris and I got up next morning, Miss Mills was cooking breakfast in the kitchenette and all the morning newspapers were piled on a coffee table in the living-room.

"Might as well read your reviews and get them over with," she called.

The coverage of Nanny Ordway's death was more or less what I'd expected it to be. The *Times* had the episode buried where it belonged in a short column on a middle page. But the less sedate publications had gone to town. One of them displayed the photograph of Iris and me, kissing at the airport, blown up on the front page under a banner headline: IRIS DULUTH FINDS DEAD GIRL IN HUSBAND'S BEDROOM. I glanced through several of the accounts. There was no photograph of Nanny. I suppose they hadn't been able to get hold of one. They had nothing except the basic fact of her death and discovery, but they played it to the hilt with as many unsavory innuendos as their legal departments had okayed.

I didn't feel quite as bad about them as I had thought I would. The exaggeration took everything out of the realm of reality where it had power to hurt. Their "brilliant" Nanny Ordway, their "beautiful" Iris Duluth, their "debonair" Peter Duluth seemed to have no connection with ourselves. They were just glamorized puppets, fabricated by journalists to make the subway ride from 125th Street to Canal a little less drab.

I wasn't hungry. But Miss Mills made us eat. In her way she was as bossy as Lottie. She was wearing a startlingly exotic red housecoat which looked odd with the pince-nez. She was just friendly enough and sarcastic enough and level-headed enough to keep us on an even keel.

Iris was determined that we should move back to the apartment. We'd have to sooner or later. Sooner was better, she thought, like getting back on a horse after it had thrown you. I agreed with her. Once we'd eaten and dressed, we all went our separate ways—Iris back to face the apartment alone, Miss Mills to hold down the office, I to the station-house and Lieutenant Trant.

As I walked down Madison Avenue through the crisp November sunshine, I was surprised at my relative serenity. No one recognized me as the monster of the headlines. Nothing in the familiar sights around me indicated change. I had conquered my night fears. Of course Nanny Ordway had not been in love with me, and I had nothing for which to blame myself.

For the first time, I felt an almost affectionate pity for her. The poor kid must have had something bad in her life about which she'd told me nothing. Perhaps, if our friendship had been a little less abortive, I might have been able to help her. But the police would discover the truth and I would be exonerated. How could I not be when I was so convinced of my freedom from guilt?

Yes, this was just a seven days' wonder. On the eighth day, another crop of juicy scandals would have obliterated ours from the public mind.

At that time I was an amateur in disaster. Because I felt steadier than the night before, I imagined I was over the hump. I never reminded myself that there are cores of calm in the center of the most raging hurricanes.

I went into the station-house, if not cheerfully, at least with a feeling of detachment, as if I were only a temporary interloper in its world of distress and doom.

I was taken upstairs through the Detectives' Room to the same office of the night before. It was empty and I was left there. A couple of newspapers were strewn on the desk. I saw my own name in a headline. I wondered if Lieutenant Trant had left the papers there on purpose to intimidate me. Probably that was just what he had done. It struck me as a pointlessly devious device. I felt a healthy indignation.

He came in soon. He was carrying a sheaf of papers, and I was surprised at the strength of my antagonism to him. He was so quiet, so polite. Even the way he held himself seemed to me that morning to have an affected modesty. His not to puff himself up! Oh, no—what was he but a humble acolyte of the Great Goddess Justice?

"Good morning, Mr. Duluth. Here are the typescripts of the statements you made last night. Care to look them over? Excuse me a moment. I'll be right with you."

He went away, leaving the typewritten sheets on the desk with the open newspapers. He was gone quite a long time. With the door shut, the little boxlike office took on once again its atmosphere of insulation. I read the two statements through three times to make sure they were correct. There it was all neatly typed up for the files—the sum total of my anomalous acquaintance with Nanny Ordway. There was nothing I could add, nothing I could subtract.

Eventually Lieutenant Trant came back with some more papers. He sat down behind the desk opposite me.

"Statements all right, Mr. Duluth?"

"They're all right."

"Nothing new occurred to you during the night?"

He said that with a veiled irony that riled me and I snapped:

"During the night I slept."

It was a foolish, irritable thing to have said. Lieutenant Trant glanced at me quickly.

"I'm glad you slept, Mr. Duluth. Nanny Ordway didn't. She was up at the morgue in Bellevue having her heart cut out."

His voice, for Lieutenant Trant, was extraordinarily harsh. It was very plain what he thought of me. Suddenly our antagonism had come to the surface.

"You are prepared to sign those statements, Mr. Duluth?"

"Of course I am."

"They represent the truth and the whole truth of your association with Nanny Ordway?"

"They do."

"There had been nothing between you—no love passages—nothing of that sort which could have caused her to kill herself? in your apartment?"

"So we're back to that again."

"Yes, we are."

"There was nothing between us—no love passages—nothing of that sort which could have caused her to kill herself in my apartment."

Lieutenant Trant pressed a buzzer on his desk. A cop put his head around the door.

"Ask Miss Amberley to step in, will you?"

The cop went away and came back with a girl, letting her through the door and closing it behind her. She was a tall girl about twenty-eight years old. She was dowdily dressed with an old tweed coat like Nanny's and black ballet slippers. She wasn't attractive. She had the eccentric look of a girl from a social family who was making it her life-work to live down her background.

"Miss Amberley," said Lieutenant Trant, "this is Mr. Duluth."

The girl barely inclined her head. Her rather prominent green eyes, shifting to me for a second, were filled with disgust. There is no other, less violent word to describe their expression. It was rather shocking.

"I don't believe you have met Mr. Duluth, Miss Amberley."

"No."

"But you've been living with Miss Ordway at 31 Charlton Street, haven't you?"

"I have."

"And last night you made a statement to me."

"I did."

"You don't mind going over some of the same ground again?"

"I don't mind."

Lieutenant Trant didn't look at me. Neither did the girl. In this quiet colloquy between these two quiet, polite people, I had no more share than my name in the newspaper headlines on the desk.

"You were on friendly terms with Miss Ordway, weren't you, Miss Amberley?"

"She was my best friend."

"And, naturally, she confided in you?"

"Of course."

"Did she ever, in the last five weeks, mention Mr. Duluth to you?"

"She did." Miss Amberley moistened her lips. That was when I noticed that she, like Nanny Ordway, was wearing no lipstick at all. "Many, many times."

"From what she said, what was your impression of the relations between them?"

"It wasn't just my impression. Nanny said it over and over again in the most specific terms."

"Said what, Miss Amberley?"

"That she was in love with him." Miss Amberley's voice quavered slightly. "And he was in love with her."

I looked at that tall, dowdy girl whom I had never seen in my life before, whom I had heard only once for one moment on a phone and, as I looked at her and the implacable chill on her face, I felt the beginnings of horror.

"For God's sake . . ." I began.

"Please, Mr. Duluth, I'd rather you didn't interrupt." Lieutenant Trant's gray gaze was fixed on Miss Amberley. "Miss Ordway told you, of course, that Mr. Duluth was a married man?"

"Of course she did. It upset her terribly. Nanny wasn't the sort that enjoyed stealing another woman's husband. To begin with, she struggled against it, but it was too strong, she said. He convinced her he needed her and, because she loved him and he came first, she decided that his wife would have to be the one to suffer."

"And Mr. Duluth had spoken about divorcing his wife?"

"Oh, yes," said Miss Amberley. "Mr. Duluth had promised to get a divorce."

I got up. I said, "Listen to me."

"Please, Mr. Duluth . . ."

"I said—listen to me." I shouted it at them. "I don't know Miss Amberley. I don't know how malicious she is. I don't know how gullible she is. But every word she's said has been a lie. Maybe they're her own lies; maybe they're Nanny Ordway's lies. I don't give a damn whose lies they are. But they are lies."

The girl stood absolutely still, ignoring me. Lieutenant Trant's eyes rested on me for a moment. Then he turned them abruptly back to Miss Amberley.

"From your many talks with your friend, Miss Amberley, did you gather whether this passion between Miss Ordway and Mr. Duluth had been of an entirely Platonic order?"

"Platonic!" Miss Amberley echoed the word explosively. "Of course it wasn't Platonic. Nanny was only a child. She pretended to be worldly-wise, but she was innocent as a babe. Do you think she was any match for a professional seducer? *This is love; this isn't just sex. Love has to be fulfilled. It's a sin not to fulfill it.* All that hogwash! Do you suppose Nanny could have stood up against it? Of course they slept together right up to the end."

The conviction in her voice, the contempt, the female fear and loathing of the male were ugly as a drawing scrawled on a wall. I felt as if a garbage truck had been spilled on me.

"I warned her," Miss Amberley's low, cultured, terrible voice was running on. "Time and time again I tried to make her see what she was letting herself in for. He'd never divorce his wife, I told her. Why should he when he was getting all he wanted on the side? We had terrible fights. She was alone in the world. I was her only friend. I was older. I knew it was up to me to help her even to the extent of losing her friendship. But what could I do?"

She swung around to glare at me and spat out, "How can a mere girl compete with a great hulk of male flesh?"

I turned to Trant and said, "This girl's a lunatic. Can't you see that? She's making all this up out of some dirty, diseased . . ."

"I asked you not to interrupt, Mr. Duluth," cut in Lieutenant Trant's soft, utterly undisturbed voice. "Miss Amberley, last night we also discussed, didn't we, Miss Ordway's behavior on the night before her death?"

"We did." Miss Amberley's voice was almost a whisper now. "That night she came home late. I'd been away for a week, visiting my family in Boston. I'd gone to bed early right off the train and I was asleep when she got back. But her typewriter woke me. I looked up from the bed and she was sitting at the desk, typing. It's just one room there. We live and sleep there in the same room. I looked up from the bed and there she was, like a ghost, like a girl who'd just been given a death sentence. I got up. I said, 'Nanny, what is it? What's happened?' She didn't answer. She just sat there, typing. She wouldn't speak, not a word. She didn't cry or anything. She was just sitting there numb. Finally she undressed and went to bed. The next morning she got up before I did. I never saw her again."

"And you attribute this change in Miss Ordway to some quarrel with Mr. Duluth? A sudden decision on his part, for example, not to ask his wife for a divorce, after all?"

"I do."

"And you think this may have been the reason for her death the next day?"

"Of course it was. Of course that's why Nanny killed herself."

I opened my mouth to speak again, but Lieutenant Trant broke in:

"Thank you, Miss Amberley. That will be all right now."

Miss Amberley started for the door.

I called after her. "Hey, you. Wait a minute."

But she opened the door, passed through it, and closed it behind her.

I spun around to Lieutenant Trant. "Get her back. You let her accuse me of seducing a young girl, making false promises to marry her, driving her to suicide. Even the Ogpu would give me a chance to come back at her. Let me talk to her. In five seconds, I'd have that story tumbling around her ears."

"You would?" Lieutenant Trant looked up at me brisk, detached, the impersonal servant of the Law. He touched the buzzer again on his desk.

"She's an obvious neurotic." I was too furious and scared to be coherent. "One of those girls with a grudge against men. My God, you're a policeman. You must have come across cases like that. You . . ."

"You're a lightning analyst of character, aren't you, Mr. Duluth? Too bad you weren't as perceptive with Nanny Ordway."

The cop was at the door again. Lieutenant Trant said, "Okay. Bring in Mrs. Coletti, Bill."

"Mrs. Coletti?" I echoed. "*Lucia* Coletti, our maid?"

"You were the one who suggested her as a corroborative witness."

"Of course I was."

Lieutenant Trant was leafing through the typewritten sheets in front of him. "In your statement, you said that Nanny Ordway came every morning to your apartment after you'd left for your office. She came there merely because you had been generous enough to loan her the apartment to write in. That's still your story, I imagine?"

"Why wouldn't it be?"

"She never, for example, spent the night?"

"If she had, I'd have told you."

"Of course, Mr. Duluth, I haven't forgotten your passion for the truth. You are on friendly terms with Lucia Coletti?"

"Very friendly."

"She has no reason to bear a grudge against you, to wish you ill?"

"For heaven's sake, no."

"Then you won't accuse her of being neurotic. Fine. At least we've got that settled."

Lucia came in. She was plump and Italian and sixtyish and normally as cheerful as a carnival. That morning in her black work coat with her black work hat jammed on her gray hair she looked thoroughly subdued. She threw me a quick, beseeching glance and then turned, oppressed and respectful, to Lieutenant Trant.

He had chosen several sheets from the pile of papers. Holding them, he looked up at her with bright friendliness.

"Good morning, Mrs. Coletti. Thank you for coming. I hope it hasn't inconvenienced you?"

"My sister—she went in my place to Miss Marin's."

"I expect you know why I've asked you to drop in. You are Mrs. Lucia Coletti. You live with your sister, Mrs. Bruno, on West Tenth Street and you work as part-time maid for Mr. and Mrs. Duluth. You and your sister were interviewed last night by myself at your home. I just want you to repeat in front of Mr. Duluth what you told me last night."

"I didn't tell you nothing." Lucia flung around to me, throwing a hand out. "Honest, Mr. Duluth, I swear it. When you give me that ten bucks not to tell Miss Marin, I promised I wouldn't say nothing. And I didn't. It was my sister. Gab, gab, gab all the time. She's stupid. She don't know from nothing. It was my sister . . ."

When she mentioned the ten dollars, Lieutenant Trant's eyes flicked up and then down. He'd taken that in and interpreted it all right. Now he interrupted:

"Your sister, Mrs. Coletti, only told me what you'd already told her. I'm sorry if this is painful to you. Perhaps it would be easier if I just read the significant part of your sister's statement out loud."

He looked down at the papers in his hand. "Mr. Duluth claims that Miss Ordway never spent the night in his apartment. He claims that she arrived every morning around ten after he himself had left. He mentioned you as someone who could back up that assertion." He paused. "I will now read part of your sister's statement. And, Mr. Duluth, I'd be obliged if you would keep quiet until I have finished."

He started to read in a flat, official voice:

LIEUTENANT TRANT: Mrs. Bruno, when your sister comes back from work in the evenings, does she, in a perfectly normal way, chat with you about the people she works for?

MRS. BRUNO: Oh, sure, sure. All the time.

LIEUTENANT TRANT: And, amongst others, has she chatted with you about Mr. and Mrs. Duluth?

MRS. BRUNO: Sure. All the time. She's crazy about Mr. and Mrs. Duluth.

LIEUTENANT TRANT: Recently did she tell you that Mrs. Duluth was away in Jamaica?

MRS. BRUNO: With her momma that was sick.

LIEUTENANT TRANT: That's it. So she told you that Mrs. Duluth was away.

MRS. BRUNO: Sure.

LIEUTENANT TRANT: After Mrs. Duluth was away, did your sister mention a girl, a young girl, a friend of Mr. Duluth's, called Ordway. Miss Nanny Ordway?

MRS. BRUNO: The little girl? My God, I should say. That one. That was a shameless one. My God, lying there in the bed sound asleep in a pair of Mrs. Duluth's pajamas, lying there with Lucia coming right in.

LIEUTENANT TRANT: Do I understand you to say

that your sister found Miss Ordway asleep in Mr. Duluth's bed, wearing a pair of his wife's pajamas?

MRS. BRUNO: Sure. Lucia, she was up in the air about it. Never seen nothing like it. And Mr. and Mrs. Duluth always getting on so good with each other.

LIEUTENANT TRANT: And Mr. Duluth was with her?

MRS. BRUNO: Him? Oh, no. Mr. Duluth wouldn't do nothing like that. He has lots of respect for Lucia. He'd gone off then. He'd left her alone.

Lieutenant Trant stopped reading and put the papers down on his desk, studiously ignoring me.

"Well, Mrs. Coletti, does that sound correct?"

Lucia had flushed a deep crimson. She stammered: "Yes, I—I guess that's what my sister said."

"And it was true, of course?"

"I guess so. Sure. It's true. I . . ." Lucia turned miserably to me. "Mr. Duluth, honest, I didn't mean to make trouble. Talking with my sister—ain't nothing wrong in that. I didn't . . ."

"All right, Mrs. Coletti." Lieutenant Trant's voice was firm and final. "That'll be all at the moment. Thank you again for dropping by."

He got up, took Lucia's elbow and guided her out of the office. He came back. He stood by the door, looking at me with complete absence of triumph on his face. That was his way of rubbing in the fact of his total victory.

"So much for your determination to tell the truth at all costs, Mr. Duluth. I'm glad you slept last night. It was, of course, the sleep of the pure and the just."

CHAPTER NINE

I was deathly afraid of Nanny Ordway then. There were other emotions, of course—anger at Lieutenant Trant's unjustified contempt of me, understanding of it, rebellious incredulity that I should have been chosen for so fantastic a dilemma, and a dim awareness that horror could lurk around the corner for everybody. But it was the fear of Nanny Ordway that predominated. She was dead. That unobtrusive, earnest little girl—"a girl and a man can be friends"—had checked out on a red scarf tied to my chandelier. But already that morning, she had arisen twice from the dead and spoken through the lips of Miss Amberley and Lucia Coletti's sister.

She had spoken and she had become terrible as a gorgon's head.

Lieutenant Trant was still looking at me. I looked back. I was pulled in too many directions to have any adequate defense. How could the Nanny Ordway whom I had foolishly and pointlessly allowed to slip into my life be the same girl who had been found by Lucia asleep in my bed, who had talked of passion and divorce to Miss Amberley and who had sat like a ghost in front of her typewriter on the night before she died?

She had been mad, of course. Mad as the four winds of heaven. And worse than merely mad. She had been maliciously mad. For the world, for me, too, she had hidden behind a plausible façade of sanity, but in secret she had been insanely plotting to destroy me along with herself. What other explanation could there be?

But who was going to believe it? Her martyred innocence had been established. There was nothing to cast doubt upon it—nothing at all except my own hopelessly discredited word.

The truth, I thought, the naked lady at the bottom of the well. Lieutenant Trant thought he had found her. He had never been wider from the mark.

Wearily, anticipating defeat, I said, "I deny it all."

"That's your privilege, Mr. Duluth."

"I deny it all not because I'm a lunatic who's determined to cling to a shipwrecked lie. I deny it because it's not true. Don't ask me what's wrong with Miss Amberley. Don't ask me what's wrong with Lucia. For God's sake, don't ask me what was wrong with Nanny Ordway. What happened, happened, and it happened the way I told you in my statement."

"You're suggesting then that Miss Ordway deliberately over a period of weeks fabricated a false story for her roommate, that she deliberately got into your bed and pretended to be asleep there to deceive the maid?"

"She was mad," I said.

"Last night you told me that she had seemed to you a perfectly normal girl."

"Seemed!" I repeated. "Do detectives care about 'seemed'? Do you always have to believe the obvious?"

"I seldom believe the obvious."

"But in this case you do?"

"In this case with two witnesses, one of them friendly to yourself, backing up the plausible obvious against the implausible unobvious, I'll settle for the obvious. Even you, Mr. Duluth, must agree that if Miss Ordway had been mad, Miss Amberley, who had roomed with her for months, would have been conscious of it. And yet . . ."

His voice ran on. I was exhausted by his stupid-clever persistence, his relentless Socratic deductions from a situation that had soared far beyond the borders of logic. I, of course, should be playing it his way. I should be demanding a cross-examination of Miss Amberley, swearing my innocence, seething with righteous indignation. But where would it get me? How, for example, could I explain away the fact that Lucia had seen Nanny Ordway in my bed? Lucia wouldn't lie. She was fond of me.

Lieutenant Trant had stopped speaking. I had no idea what he had been talking about, but he was waiting for an answer.

I said, "Do we have to go on with this conversation? I know what you think of me. I know I'm never going to change your opinion. I'm not even interested in trying. After all, I'm not married to you. Just tell me the set-up—the police set-up. Are you going to arrest me? If not—for God's sake, let me sign those statements and get out of here."

His eyes widened slightly. I could see white all around his irises. "You still want to sign those statements?"

"Don't you listen to a word I say?"

"Okay, Mr. Duluth." He shrugged. It was the shrug of a man confronted with behavior beyond belief and beneath any further consideration. "You may sign the statements."

"And I'm not under arrest?"

"Why should you be under arrest, Mr. Duluth?"

"As a wicked, wicked liar, a heartless seducer of innocent young girls, and a cynical devil-may-care."

Lieutenant Trant flushed. I was vaguely surprised

that his blood and skin were human enough to permit such a frailty. He gestured to the desk. "Sign your statements, Mr. Duluth."

I went to the desk. I scrawled my signature at the end of the two documents. I went back and initialed each individual page. I took a savage delight in it as if I were throwing a gauntlet in Lieutenant Trant's incorruptibly noble face and in the face of all insensitive jumpers at conclusions.

"Okay." I got up. "Anything else?"

"Nothing at the moment, Mr. Duluth." Lieutenant Trant picked up the statements, rustling through the papers, checking the signatures. "The full autopsy reports are not in yet. Those things take time, you know. Two or three days."

He looked up from the papers. "But, for your information, Miss Ordway died between two-thirty and four —just about the time that you were alone at the moviehouse. If there should turn out to be a reason for continuing the investigation, that is where I would start— by checking on your alibi."

"I'm sure you would." I held out my hand, automatically, I suppose, because that's what you do when you leave someone. "I'm delighted that Nanny Ordway has a champion, Lieutenant. Too bad she wasn't your little friend instead of mine. You would have enjoyed the experience."

As I left the office, I wondered who was the more pathetic, I with my brand of stupidity or Lieutenant Trant with his.

I hurried through the Detectives' Room and down to the street. Immediately I was surrounded by reporters. There were about six of them and they were hot on the trail.

"Hey, Mr. Duluth, do you know a Miss Amberley?"

"Yes."

"Want to hear a statement Miss Amberley just made to us?"

"No."

"Heck, Mr. Duluth, aren't you going to deny Miss Amberley's statement?"

A taxi was cruising by. I flagged it and escaped. Maybe I should have said something to the reporters. But I couldn't just then. I wanted a drink. Dimly I realized that I hadn't wanted a drink that badly that early in the day for many years.

"Where to?" asked the driver.

I gave the office address. I had intended to go straight back to Iris, but I realized how much was now going to depend on what I said to her. Until then, she had believed me. But that had been before Miss Amberley and Lucia's sister. I felt the need for Miss Mills' bolstering sanity. If I could get Miss Mills to believe me, that would be something. It would help overcome the feeling that I was an outcast, that all the world was lined up against me along with Lieutenant Trant, Miss Amberley, and Mrs. Bruno.

The goldfish feeling was in the office. The girl at the reception desk had it in her eyes as she said: Good morning, Mr. Duluth. The other secretary, bustling around with papers, had it as well. It only dissolved in Miss Mills' office. I found her leaning back in her chair with her legs up on the desk, reading her mail.

"Well, back from the wars."

"Bloody," I said, "and bowed."

She looked at me a moment in silence. Then she reached down and pulled a bottle of rye from a drawer in the desk.

"Emergency."

She poured two shots, one for me, one for herself. I told her my version of the story. Then I told her everything that Miss Amberley had said, everything that Mrs. Bruno had been quoted as saying—and all Lieutenant Trant's moral and edifying comments.

I hated telling it, not so much because it made me sound like a futile, cowardly liar, but because it brought Nanny Ordway near again. I could almost hear the rustle of Miss Amberley's blue satin evening gown, almost see the hair tumbling forward over the naïve, quiet little face. Nanny Ordway—the harmless water-nymph who had died and become a fury, stalking my marriage, my career, and my peace of mind.

It was the marriage that mattered most, of course. Without Iris, the rest didn't count.

I finished. I said, "You saw her once. Here in the office."

"Sure. Miss O'Dream."

"I know what that sounds like. Miss O'Dream— Daddy Duluth. I know what everything sounds like. But I never touched her. I swear it. All that about the bed, about protestations of marriage and divorce—she was stark, staring mad. She . . ." I broke off. The drink wasn't helping. "Is Iris going to believe me?"

Miss Mills didn't answer for a moment. Then she said: "Lottie wouldn't believe a story like that from Brian."

"Of course she wouldn't. But Iris . . ."

"Lottie just owns Brian, but Iris loves you. That helps, I guess?"

"You guess?"

"Maybe it helps. Maybe it makes it harder. I wouldn't know. I'm not up on the love department on account of looking like a pig. It's a matter for Iris and you. Tell her, and pray that she's about five hundred per cent more trusting than most females."

That wasn't as encouraging as I had hoped. "And you, Miss Mills. Do you believe me?"

"I believe that men can be fools and women can be bitches. I also believe that women can be crazy."

"Even when they seem to the world to be nice, well-intended little girls?"

Miss Mills smiled. "I believe the world can be a fool too."

I said, "Then you do believe me?"

She leaned across the desk and put her hand on mine. "It doesn't matter one hoot in hell to you, darling, whether I believe you or not. But I probably do. I'm the greatest believer of all time. That's one of my many assets. Now run along and tell Iris. I'll keep my fingers crossed."

CHAPTER TEN

I left the office and took a taxi home. I saw what a fool I had been to expect Miss Mills to work another miracle. I was out of diapers now. Nursey couldn't help any more. I was on my own. As the taxi dropped me outside our door, I felt panicked. It seemed incredible that I could be afraid of Iris, that things could have changed that much.

I let myself into the apartment. Immediately I heard an all-too-familiar voice. It wasn't Iris' voice. It was loud and beautiful and it was booming like surf on a rocky shore.

Iris was sitting on the couch in the living-room, smoking a cigarette. Lottie was pacing up and down the center of the rug. When she saw me, she broke off in mid-sentence and spun around to me, all the venom of all the asps in the world in her eyes.

"Well!" she said. "The hunter is home from the hills."

Iris got up. "Lottie, dear, run along and leave us."

"Leave you!" Lottie snorted. "The only person who should be left—quickly and finally with full process of law—is Peter Duluth. That is, unless you want a succession of little girls asleep in your bed every morning and hanging from your chandelier every night."

She flounced toward me—Oatfields, Wisconsin, warming up for the lynching-bee.

"I don't mind, of course, Peter, *dear*, that you cause

havoc in my household by dragging my maid from police station to police station when she should have been dusting. I don't mind that in the least. After all, it was most instructive to meet Lucia's sister. Quite a girl, Mrs. Bruno—with a salty gift for narrative. It cost you ten bucks to keep Lucia from telling me about your cheap little affair, didn't it? You should have invested another ten bucks in her sister."

I couldn't bear the sight of her. Wasn't she married? Didn't she have a man of her own? Why couldn't she use Brian for her emotional setting-up exercises?

"Oh, shut up, Lottie," I said.

"Shut up? Just try to shut me up. Try to shut the world up! What are you going to do? Gag Colonel Mc-Cormick? Smother the whole Hearst chain? Strangle Mr. Sulzberger in his sleep?" She swung back and ran to Iris, enveloping her in her arms. "Iris, my darling Iris, I implore you. I plead with you. For your own sake, don't let him talk you around. Don't listen to his dirty, ingenious self-justifications. You're not a little mole—a little mole of a wife who has to put up with things like this. Get rid of him. Just leave a couple of pairs of your old pajamas around and a noose or two—that'll be enough to satisfy him."

"Get out, Lottie," I said.

She released Iris and swept toward me. "Don't you worry. I'm getting out of here. To think that I trusted you! To think that I killed myself last night at the theater trying to persuade all those poor, misguided people that you had been grievously wronged! But there's one thing, Peter. Yes, there's one thing. So long as I'm playing at that theater, don't you dare come anywhere near it. Don't you dare."

She reached the door. She turned, tossing Iris a butterfly kiss. "Remember, darling. The moment it's settled, come up to us. Brian agrees with me. He's dying to have you—for as long as you want to stay. *We* are your friends."

She slammed the door. Act one—curtain.

Iris and I looked at each other. It was too horrible not to be a bit funny.

I said, "I've finally done what you wanted me to do. I've mortally offended Lottie."

She didn't smile. I hadn't expected her to.

She said, "Is it over at the police station?"

"Yes."

"The suicide's been established and everything?"

"I guess so. The official autopsy report's not in yet."

"Of course Lieutenant Trant knows all this about Lucia and her sister?"

"Of course." I paused. "That isn't the half of it."

I told her about Miss Amberley. I wasn't as panicked as I had been. I suppose Iris was such a basic part of my life that her presence, even at this of all times, was automatically steadying. Not that she helped me. While I talked, she just sat there on the couch with no visible change of expression. Usually I could tell what she was thinking as if I was thinking it myself. But that day I couldn't tell.

I realized how hard it was for her. I wasn't so much of a fool as to imagine she would believe me just because she loved me. Nobody does that outside of the movies. Miss Mills was right. Because she loved me, it was probably tougher for her. When you love someone, there's always part of you that expects the worst because it dreads the worst.

But she'd want to believe me. That I knew. She'd believe me if she could.

When I finished, she said, "That's all?"

"Yes."

"And Lieutenant Trant isn't going to bother you any more?"

"He would if he could."

She crossed to the bar for a cigarette and lit it. Usually her beauty made me proud and self-assured because she was my wife. Now the beauty and my desire to touch her were blighted by the possibility of losing her.

"Did you really give Lucia ten dollars not to tell Lottie?"

"Yes. I did."

"Why?"

"God, you know Lottie. If she'd found out I'd given Nanny a key, she'd have plunged into Pinero up to her neckline."

"You didn't write to me about it either."

"No. I meant to. I guess—well, in the back of my mind, I guess I felt I was being a fool about the whole thing."

Iris still wasn't looking at me. "And you don't have any explanation for why Lucia found her asleep in our bed, wearing my pajamas."

"Just that she was mad."

"Even if she'd been mad, she'd have had to have some reason."

I tried: "She was kind of Cinderella-ish about wealth, comfort, things like that. Maybe she had a whim and wanted to find out how it felt to be in a rather grand bed in rather grand pajamas." That sounded the thinnest of all my protestations. "She just could have felt that way. And then, after Lucia had caught her, she could have felt foolish, unable to bring herself to explain. Maybe it was that. I know, when I lent her your evening dress . . ."

Iris looked up then. "When you—what, Peter?"

"Didn't I tell you? When I took her to the theater?

It was the last minute. She didn't have time to go home and change. I let her put on one of your dresses."

"I see."

I don't think Iris had the slightest realization that she was adopting Lieutenant Trant's favorite phrase. I began to feel jittery and even more of a heel.

"I seem to have made a mess of it all the way around."

"Oh, it's a mess. Of course it's a mess." Iris put down her cigarette. "And all the rest, all the stuff the roommate said—you can't see any explanation for that—except that Nanny Ordway was mad."

"That's all, I guess."

"There are girls like that. Everyone knows. Girls who live in a dream world, who believe their own fantasies, who can do more damage than an armored division."

She broke off. I could see her dilemma with agonizing clarity. It wasn't just the outside evidence against me. It was my own behavior which seemed so damaging. My idiotic secrecy. Why hadn't I written to Iris about the key? Why had I given Lucia ten dollars? My inexplicable generosity. Why had I picked Nanny Ordway from all the girls in New York to patronize? Why had I been so crazy as to lend her Iris' dress?

I said, "Can you believe me? I don't blame you if you can't."

She was studying my face as if, like Lieutenant Trant, she thought she could read the truth there. Maybe she could see more than Lieutenant Trant. Very quietly, she said:

"Last night I realized it wasn't any good being in the middle, half believing, half not believing. And then, when Lieutenant Trant was so clever, and veiled and merciless . . . I believed you, Peter. I've started now. I'm not going to stop yet. She was mad. Of course, she was mad."

I had grown so used to being kicked around. It was difficult to grasp the fact that the only important thing was going to be all right.

I hurried to her. She put her arms around me and clung to me as if it were she and not I who needed comforting.

"Oh, Peter, I don't want to be a stinker. I don't want to be like Lottie. If I can't trust you, what can I trust?"

"Baby . . ."

"It's all right. I'll be all right in a minute."

I kissed her. I kept her in my arms. She was beautiful and good—far too good for me. I felt humble and grateful, but I was stable again.

"Iris, darling . . ."

"That Lottie!" She turned her face up to mine. Somehow she was managing to smile. "I'd give my last cent to have her find Brian in bed with a set of quintuplets—all five of them wearing her pajamas."

"The Chinese ones," I said, "with the pagodas across the bosom."

CHAPTER ELEVEN

The fact that my wife was standing by me should have brought some sort of release from pressure. But this was another miracle that didn't quite come off. Almost immediately a constraint began to develop between us. Neither of us admitted it, but it was there. We didn't, for example, mention Nanny Ordway again, which in itself was a proof that we were afraid. Iris' belief in me was too fragile; my own sense of blamelessness too insecure.

We went out to lunch together. We weren't bothered much by the goldfish treatment. After lunch, we went back to the apartment. The press called all the time. So did a lot of people I knew in the Theater. Their commiserations didn't help. They thought they were being friendly but they were really being nosy. The afternoon papers came out with Miss Amberley's statement. It wasn't quite as bad as I had expected. Most of her vindictive bitterness had been blue-penciled. But the essential fact was there. *Nanny Ordway's Roommate Tells Of Thwarted Love.* There were still no photographs of Nanny which made it easier for the copy-writers. Now she wasn't only a "brilliant young writer," she was also an "exotic brunette." It was all suggestive enough to satisfy the most respectable of readers.

Alec Ryder called up and invited us to dinner. We accepted because, oddly enough, we didn't know what else to do. While we were waiting for him to pick us up, Brian came down from upstairs. He looked very unhappy.

"Lottie's gone to the theater. I thought . . . heck, I just wanted to tell you not to worry about Lottie, Peter. You know her. She flies off the handle. But she'll come around when she's got it out of her system. That policeman was around this morning, you know, checking. She could have blown her top to him. But she didn't. She clammed right up. Lottie's okay really."

He grinned shyly at Iris. "As for me, I say to hell with Nanny Ordway. Iris, if you were a man and had been around, you'd have known kids like that. They come a dime a dozen. Nuts—nuttier than a fruitcake. The roommate too. Both of them . . ." He put his hand on her arm. "Don't take it out on Peter, uh?"

That was decent of him. We invited him in for a drink, but he had to go to the theater. Lottie always did the *London Times* crossword puzzle in her dressing-room. She'd called to say she'd forgotten it. Brian had to tote it.

When Alec arrived, he turned out to be just the right person. He was English enough and smooth enough to act as if he'd never heard of Nanny Ordway and, although I knew he was itching to sell Iris on the London trip, he didn't bring it up once. He spent most of dinner talking about his wife's success in a new play that had just opened in the West End. He was a nice guy too.

But nothing could have saved the evening. We'd drunk a few cocktails before dinner and brandy afterwards. By the time we got home it was around eleven o'clock. The drink had only aggravated my nervous tension. The apartment, indelibly marked now with the memory of Nanny Ordway, seemed gloomy as a funeral parlor. As we entered it, I glanced at Iris. She had been silent ever since we left Alec. She looked pale and rather severe. In my over-sensitive state, it seemed to me she was being martyrish and I snapped:

"There's no need to be noble and forgiving. I'm not the Great Sinner—remember?"

It was an unattractive thing to have said. I knew it. I wished I hadn't said it, but I hadn't been able to stop myself.

She sat down wearily on the couch. "I'm not being forgiving, Peter."

I felt ashamed. I sat down next to her. "I'm sorry, baby. It's just that . . . I feel like hell."

"I don't feel any too radiant myself."

I thought of mixing us a drink and decided not to. "You do believe me, don't you?"

"Yes, dear."

"If you don't, I wish you'd say so. I'd much rather . . ."

"Peter, please."

"But I mean it. I can't stand thinking of you as a sort of elaborate Penelope . . ."

"Shut up, Peter." She looked at me fiercely. "Don't you see you're only making it harder?"

"Then you don't believe me."

"I didn't say so."

"But you think so. You're just being large-scale and sophisticated and mellow. Poor Peter had his little fling. Maybe it was more or less innocent. Maybe the girl was just a teensy bit crazy. But men are men. It's their nature to make fools of themselves. Let's just forget about it. After all, the girl's cut down from the chandelier now. She won't get in the way when we cross to the closet."

I got up again. I didn't have much control over what I was saying. I didn't know what had hit me.

Iris got up too. "Peter, really!"

I swung around to her. The perverse desire to hurt and be hurt had me completely in its grip. "Why don't you bawl me out? Why don't you ask me what right I had messing around with a girl young enough to be my own daughter? Why don't you rub it in that you came all the way back from Jamaica, that you walked into your own bedroom and you found . . . Isn't it about time?"

She was angry too, infected with the same excited, unreal anger as mine. "All right, Peter. If you want it that way. I don't see why the hell you lent her my dress."

"Your dress?"

"You've already forgotten, haven't you? That's how insensitive you are."

"But . . ."

"I suppose you'd like it if you came back and discovered I'd dressed some little boy up in your Bronzini bathrobe."

"I wouldn't give a damn."

"And I'm not saying anything about my pajamas. I'm not saying anything about that. Or about the ten dollars to Lucia. Or . . ."

"Now it's coming out," I broke in. "Now you've proved you don't believe me."

We stood looking at each other. Now that I'd triumphed and forced things to go my way, I felt bleak as February.

"Iris, I'm sorry."

"Peter."

"Baby, I'm sorry."

We went to bed. I pretended not to care about the chandelier looming above us, but I did. There was a kind of reconciliation, but the Fury was still stalking.

Long afterwards we were both pretending to be asleep when we were really wide awake.

When I woke up next morning, Iris wasn't in the bed. I had a sudden unreasonable fear that it was all over and she had left me. I put on my robe and ran out of the bedroom. I found her. She was in the kitchen, fixing breakfast. My relief was as exaggerated as my earlier anxiety. Seeing her opening the ice-box took me back to the time before my breakfasts with Lottie and Brian, to that dim period when a day had been nothing more complicated than a pleasant succession of twenty-four hours.

"Good morning, Peter."

"Good morning."

I kissed her. Normally I would have told her of my absurd delusion, but, although her kiss felt no different, my instinct warned me against it. That was when I remembered again the delicate balance of confidence between us.

"Take your shower, darling," she said. "Then we'll be ready."

I went to the bathroom and showered. I tried to think about the day ahead of us. Should I treat it as just an ordinary day? Should I go to the office and Miss Mills and continue with plans for *Let Live* as if nothing had happened? What did one do about an episode which had been officially closed by the police? Wasn't it best to try to close it too in my mind, even though none of it, least of all the role I had played, was understandable at all? Hadn't Nanny Ordway taken the place of Lieutenant Trant as The Enemy? Wasn't the best way to defeat her to forget her? There would be reporters, of course, and Lottie with her melodramatic veto on my entering the *Star Rising* theater. But all of that was on the outside.

It depended on Iris, I decided. I would do whatever made it easier for her.

I dried myself, put on my robe again and went out into the living-room.

Iris was standing by the window. The elevator man must have brought up the mail. She had a bunch of letters in one hand. In the other, she had an opened letter which she was reading. She didn't hear me come in. She was completely absorbed with what she was reading.

I said, "Is breakfast ready?"

She looked up suddenly. I was shocked at the expression on her face. She looked as if a doctor had just told her she was suffering from an incurable disease.

Her mother, I thought. Bad news from her mother. "Baby, what is it?"

She didn't reply. She looked down again at the letter and then held it out to me.

"What is it?"

She took an opened envelope from her other hand and held it out too. I accepted them both. I looked first at the envelope. It had her name and her Jamaica address typed on it. The Jamaica address had been scratched out and the letter had been forwarded back to her in New York.

I let the envelope drop on the floor. I read the letter. It was typed too. It was very long. It said:

My dear Iris:

It seems all right to call you Iris. I hope you don't mind. Please, please, don't mind, because it's so important for me that you shouldn't mind anything connected with me. I know this is going to be hard for you. Heaven knows, it's hard for me. Lots of people, I guess, would say it was wrong of me to write at all. Certainly, that would be the easy thing. But, Iris, I can't do it that way. Always, ever since I was a kid, I've believed that it's honesty that matters. Somehow I have the feeling that you're the same—and that, in the long run, you stand a better chance of being happy with Peter if you know and understand and forgive than if I'd "protected" you and thereby, in a way, made a fool of you."

I glanced up at Iris. She was still standing there holding the other letters. My mouth felt dry and sour. I thought: And I was figuring what to do about today as if something new was beginning. I'd imagined the past had done its worst, that the dreadful voice from the morgue had spoken for the last time.

I went on reading.

Iris, I'm not going to tell you all the details. They are terribly, beautifully important to me, but to you they'd seem banal, tawdry, unattractive, perhaps. It's just the core of it that I want you to know. Peter and I fell in love. Oh, I fell in love. Falling! What a funny word, when really it's rising, soaring. Rising in love, they should say. I rose in love with Peter—the first moment we met. And, I think, in his way, he rose in love with me too. Oh, I'm not going to pretend it was as deep a love as mine. Men aren't like us, are they? I think maybe he was lonely without you, maybe he was a little flattered that I was younger. I think there were all sorts of other factors with him. But it happened quickly, magically, just like that. And, for a while, a wonderful while, both of us were able to forget about you. Half able, I should say, because I know that often I used to think of you at the strangest moments, with a kind of awe and a kind of love, a kind of anguished tenderness as if you'd been my very best friend instead of someone I had never even met.

And it's you, Iris dear, who has won in the end. That's why I'm writing this, of course. Because Peter and I are both of us decent people. Whatever we may have thought about ourselves, we've discovered that now. Suddenly, without any warning, it came to us both at the same time. IRIS. Even in that, you see, we had a strange sort of mutuality as if his thoughts and mine were the same. Perhaps that was why it could never really have been right between Peter and me. We were too nearly the same person. Abiding love needs a contrast, doesn't it? Doesn't it? That's what I'm telling myself now that I'm so full of unhappiness, anxiety and torment for what I have decided must happen.

Because it was I, Iris, who actually decided we must break. Peter probably felt it too, but just because he's Peter, he couldn't have found enough courage to hurt me by bringing it up himself. It was last night when we were talking about Martin. Funny, isn't it, that it was Martin who really brought you and Peter back together again? I thought of all you'd been through in Mexico. I thought of how much you must have struggled to get back together in confidence and repaired love and I thought: I'm *not* going to be another Martin. Life can't be that cheap and spiteful. It shouldn't make you "pay" in a corny Biblical sense for what you made Peter suffer in the past.

So there it is. It's over. I'm never going to see Peter again. I'm not fighting you. I'm not, *not* a rival. He's yours. And I feel, I know, I'm certain that it is you he really belongs to. You must make him believe it.

This is the hardest letter I have ever written and I know that Peter will never forgive me for it. But may I end—with my love?

NANNY ORDWAY

I looked up from the letter. It was so much worse than anything I could have imagined. It didn't sound mad; it didn't sound vindictive; it sounded like the sincere, heartbreaking confession of a very nice girl.

And, of course, beyond everything, it sounded true.

I knew I would have to fight this dreadful "sincerity" with a weapon that was equally strong. But the great crises never seem to bring the right moods. I felt weak and sick as if the poison of the letter had entered my veins.

I said, "It's all a pack of crazy lies."

"Lies." Iris' voice was very soft. "Lies, lies, lies. Miss Amberley's lying, Lucia's lying. Nanny Ordway's lying. Everyone's lying except . . ."

She broke off. I longed to cross to her and take her in my arms. The physical feeling between us might still have saved the situation. But I knew now, from looking at her white, set face, that she wouldn't let me touch her.

"Iris, baby, listen to me."

"I'm listening."

"She was crazy. We know that now. She's hounding me. She's making me pay."

"For what?"

"God, if I knew. Maybe for not falling in love with her."

"But you said she wasn't in love with you."

"I thought she wasn't."

"Thought!"

There was a moment of silence, terrible to me as an explosion. Why did I still feel guilty? What was this monstrous power in Nanny Ordway that could always half convince me of my culpability? Did I want to be a victim? Was that why I stood there, watching Nanny's poison do its work on Iris, watching with no power to produce an effective antidote?

"Iris."

"And Martin." She turned suddenly. "How did she know about Martin?"

It was all too confused in my mind now for me to remember anything coherently.

"I—I don't know."

"You must have talked to her about Martin."

"Maybe I did. Yes, that's right. One evening, we were talking. I mentioned his name."

"You mentioned his name! There you were sitting quietly with your quiet little protégé, chatting, oh so innocently, and you just happened to mention Martin. By the way, my wife had a lover once. It would amuse you to hear about him."

"It wasn't like that. I forget just how it was, but . . ."

She crossed to a chair and sat down. She brought up her hands to cover her face. That classic gesture of suffering gave me a kind of courage. I went to her and dropped down at her side.

"Baby . . ."

My hand touched her arm. She shook it off savagely.

"No, Peter . . ."

"We were talking about love. Just a stupid, kiddish talk about people and the way they love each other, how they could fall out of love and in again and . . . and I just mentioned Martin to prove . . ."

My self-defense trailed off. It had died of anemia.

How could I possibly have spoken to Nanny Ordway about Martin? I no longer could understand. That it had seemed natural and blameless at the time, I was sure. But I could never make that sound convincing now.

"Iris, don't you see? She's twisted everything. She's used every little thing that happened and misconstrued it. I don't know why. I can't imagine why. But that's what she's done."

I stayed there at her side as if being a little nearer to her physically could somehow help diminish the distance between us.

"I love you, baby. I swear I love you."

"No, Peter. Please, please no . . ."

"But, Iris . . ."

"I tried," she said. "God knows, I tried."

There was no mistaking the finality in her voice. It was someone speaking about the past. I felt cold and hollow.

I said, "You're not going to try any longer?"

She took her hands from her face and looked at me. It wasn't a look of hatred or anger. It was worse. It was a look of despair.

"I can't stay here, Peter."

What was the use of arguing? When you're knocked out, you're knocked out. You don't get up again after the count and start to fight again.

"Okay," I said.

"I don't accuse you of anything. I—I don't feel hateful. It's just that I can't stay."

I no longer seemed to have any personal emotions. All I felt was pity and tenderness for her.

"Honey, you do what you think's best."

"If I could help you, I'd stay. I would. But—but you see I can't help just now. I—It would only make it worse for you, my being here—now. It would. It . . ."

"Baby don't beat yourself up about it. Please."

She rose. "I'll be all right later, I'm sure. Just—if I go away for a while. Maybe I'll be able to see more clearly. I'll take the letter with me. I'll try to understand."

"Why don't you go to Miss Mills?"

"I'd rather be alone."

The back door buzzer sounded from the kitchen. Iris started and glanced around desperately.

"Please, Peter, you answer it."

I went out into the kitchen and opened the door. Lucia was standing there in her black work coat and black work hat. She looked awkward and unhappy.

"I got my key but I figured I'd ring. I figured—maybe you wouldn't want me to work here no more, not after all the trouble. I figured . . ."

"It's all right, Lucia." Why take it out on her? "Of course we want you to go on working."

Her face broke into a shy smile. "That's fine, Mr. Duluth. I just finished up to Miss Marin's. I thought . . . Gee, I feel terrible. I wouldn't ever . . ."

She slipped her large black purse down her arm, opened it, fumbled in it and brought out a ten dollar bill. She held it out to me.

"Here, Mr. Duluth. I want you to take this back."

I looked at the bill.

"The ten bucks you give me. I'm not going to keep it. Not after what I done."

"That's okay, Lucia."

"It isn't okay, Mr. Duluth. I wouldn't feel right. You've always been good to me." She thrust the bill stubbornly forward. "I want you to have it. I'm serious. I'm not going to keep it."

I took the bill and put it in my pocket. "All right. Thanks a lot, Lucia."

I left her in the kitchen, taking off her coat, and went back to the living-room. Iris wasn't there. I found her in the bedroom. A suitcase was open on the bed and she was packing it.

"It was Lucia," I said. "She didn't know whether we'd want her any more or not. I said yes."

"I'm glad."

She went on packing.

"You don't want to talk to her? Ask her about what she saw? Maybe . . ."

"No, Peter. No. I don't think so. Not now."

I'd reached the nadir of unhappiness. Nothing could make it worse.

"Where are you going?" I said.

"To some hotel—some little hotel. I'll not use my name. No one need know. It needn't make any fuss in the papers."

"I'll go with you in the taxi."

There was a framed photograph of me on a table by the window. She went to it, picked it up and put it on top of her clothes. Then she shut the suitcase.

We stood looking at each other. Above us was the chandelier.

"If I wasn't so mixed up, Peter . . ."

"I know."

"You'll be all right?"

"Sure."

"I—know I'll be back soon."

"I know."

I picked up the suitcase. In the kitchen, I could hear Lucia clattering dishes. We went down to the street. It was a bright morning with the air clean as country air. A taxi took us to a small uptown hotel where Iris' mother sometimes stayed.

I left Iris at the entrance and took the same taxi home.

In the cab I started to feel again. The anesthesia was wearing off. Iris said she'd be back soon. Why would she be back soon? How was she ever going to make herself believe that black was white?

Nanny Ordway had lost me my wife.

CHAPTER TWELVE

When I let myself into the apartment, Lottie was in the living-room. Oh, no, I thought. No. Anyone in the world but Lottie. She was wearing her morning lounging pajamas—shrill red, shrill chartreuse, pagodas.

She came bustling toward me.

"Where is she? Where's Iris? Lucia says you went out with a suitcase. Where is she?"

I felt weak in the knees. I sat down on the arm of a chair. "She's gone away."

"Oh! So she took my advice."

"She didn't take your goddam advice. She's just gone away for a while."

"Where is she?"

"I'm not going to tell you."

"Why didn't she come to us—to Brian and me?"

"Because she didn't want to."

"But that's absurd. Of course she'd want to. The poor, poor darling. Tell me where she is. I must call at once. I must . . ."

I got up from the chair. I said, "You're going to leave her alone."

"Alone? Leave the poor darling alone without anyone to comfort her?"

I looked at her. That energy! That vitality! That bull-dozer dressed as a woman! I made a gesture of disgust with my hand and crossed to the bar. I didn't really want a drink but I knew it would make her mad. That's what I wanted her to be.

I picked up a bottle of rye. She ran to me, catching at my sleeve.

"Peter, Peter, darling, how terrible you must feel."

"That's right."

She took the bottle away from me and put it down again on the bar. Her hands came up to my arms. They were small hands, like little white birds. On the stage Lottie gave the impression of being frail, but she's like steel really. The hands were fluttering up and down my arm. Her face was all puckered with concern.

"Peter, don't take it so hard."

"Okay."

"Darling, I'm so sorry."

"Gee, that's fine."

"Aren't I your friend? Aren't I your best friend?"

"Sure. There's nothing like a best friend for busting up marriages."

"Peter, how can you say that?"

"Hell," I said.

"Peter, dearest, you must understand." Her voice was honeyed, wheedling. "I'm Iris' friend too. When a thing like this happens, I have to think of Iris first. I have to think of the innocent one. I have to see that she does the right thing for herself. But that doesn't mean . . . Peter, you darling, that doesn't mean I would turn against you. I was saying to Brian only just now . . . That's why I came down. I was saying: Wouldn't it be better for Peter to come up to us? Iris can stay in the apartment. Iris is strong. She can look after herself. But Peter'll be jittery, all shot. He needs his friends. He really needs his friends. I said . . ."

She went on yakking. I supposed she probably meant it all. It wasn't any moment to plumb the depths of

Lottie's peculiar affections for Iris and me. I didn't care whether she meant it or not. I just knew I didn't want that insistent voice, I didn't want that insistent face, I didn't want that insistent body in the room. I wanted to be alone, or dead.

I swung around to her. "Get out of here, Lottie. Get out and stay out."

"But, Peter . . ."

"I'm fed up with your meddling. I'm fed up with you pushing your nose in where you don't belong. You're a stupid, messy woman and I don't give a damn if I never see you again. Now get out."

"Peter!" Her face crimsoned with shock, astonishment, outraged sentiment. "Really, after all I've done for you!"

"After all you've done for me?" I laughed at her full in the face. "What the hell have you done for me? What . . . ? oh, skip it. Who cares?"

"Skip it? Don't worry. I'll skip it. If you don't have the decency to recognize a kind impulse when you see it— I wash my hands. I just wash my hands." She stamped her foot. "I would have thought a man who'd betrayed his wife, seduced a young girl, driven her to suicide . . . might have been a little grateful that his friends were ready to stand by him. That's what I thought. I was wrong, as usual, of course. I suppose I'm wrong about everything. I suppose you're as innocent as a fleecy white lamb. I suppose someone murdered the wretched girl, dragged her in here and tied her to your chandelier just to vex you. You poor misjudged creature!"

She flounced to the door, tugged it open, and then turned back. The old, outworn Lottie device.

"I've done my best, Peter. This is the end. And you'd better watch out or, contract or no contract, I walk right out of the play—never to come back."

The door slammed. I sat down on the couch. My head was aching. I put my face in my hands and, as I did so, I thought: Now I'm doing it too. When things get really bad, you slip into the cliché. I must remember that next time I'm directing a play.

Lucia came in from the bedroom with the vacuum cleaner.

"She gone—Miss Marin gone?"

"Yes."

"Don't you pay no attention to her, Mr. Duluth. Blow, blow, blow. I never pay her no attention."

"Thanks, Lucia."

"I'm through in the bedroom. Okay if I start in here with the cleaner?"

"Okay."

She came toward me, gripping the cleaner in a large hand. Awkwardly, she said, "Mrs. Duluth ain't walked out on you, has she?"

"I suppose she has—for a while."

"Not on account of what I said?"

"There were a lot of other things." I glanced at her and asked, not that it mattered now. "Just what did you see that day, Lucia?"

I could tell that she wanted to talk about it and get it off her chest. "It was just like what the detective said, Mr. Duluth. I came down from Miss Marin's. I let myself in with my key like always. The other times, the girl, she was always there at the desk, beating that typewriter. But that day she wasn't. I said to myself: Where is she? Maybe she ain't coming no more. I went into the bedroom to fix the bed. There she was—sound asleep in the bed."

I could see it all as if I were the one walking into the bedroom.

"Did she wake up?"

"No, sir. No sooner I seen her, I skipped out again real quiet and went into the kitchen and started clattering the dishes around. She must have woke up right quick and snapped into it. When I was through in the kitchen and come in here, there she was just like always beating away at the typewriter, calling out: Good morning, Lucia, just like there'd been nothing different. Later I found the pajamas. They were put away in a drawer, all folded real neat. If it wasn't for the wrinkles in the pants legs, you'd never have told anything. It was almost like I'd made it all up in my mind."

But she hadn't. "That day, did you come down from Miss Marin's any earlier than usual?"

"No. Just about the same time, I guess. Ten-thirty—eleven."

"When was this?"

"Oh, a couple of days before—it happened."

"And you'd never seen anything like that before?"

"No. Nothing."

"And she never said anything?"

"No, sir. Not a thing. Not her."

I said: "It wasn't the way you think. I never had anything to do with her. She was crazy."

Lucia's tongue came out to moisten her lips. "Sure. Sure, it was like you say. A terrible thing. Mr. Duluth, is it okay if I start with the cleaner? It's kind of late."

She hadn't believed me. Her warm-hearted Italian nature didn't hold me any ill-will for what she thought I'd done, but my feeble self-defense was embarrassing her.

"Of course," I said.

I got up and went into the bedroom. Lucia had made the bed. I lay down on it. I thought lying down might help my headache. What else did I have to do anyway? Lottie would probably never forgive me for calling her a stupid, messy woman, or for laughing at her. She hated being laughed at more than anything in the world. Maybe she would seriously try to break her contract. She'd done it once before when she'd fought with a producer. If she left *Star Rising,* it would fold in a week. Lottie was the whole play. I didn't even have an understudy. The sensible thing would be to go upstairs right away, to purr over her, to tell her what a wonderful friend she was and how only she could soothe my aching breast. But I wasn't going through all that crap. It just wasn't worth it.

An image of Nanny Ordway rose in my mind— Nanny as described by Miss Amberley on the night before her death, sitting like a statue in front of her typewriter, tap, tap, tapping. Hadn't she said to me that night when she left the apartment that she still had work to do? Had that work been the letter to Iris which had irrevocably proved me a heel and a liar?

What could have been in her mind? Iris was right when she had said that even a crazy person had to have motives. Could Nanny Ordway, in her self-created fantasy world, really have kidded herself I was in love with her? Had she managed to make herself believe all the stories she had told Miss Amberley? Could she have lain there in my bed in Iris' pajamas dreaming that I was with her until the dream seemed true? Had the letter to Iris, then, been written, not in spite, but in a mad decision to bring an imaginary romance to a heroic end in renunciation and suicide?

The secret of death . . . !

I would have to solve it. My life would never be livable until I had understood what had wrecked it. Nor would there be any hope of a true reconciliation with Iris.

Suddenly, the bedroom, doubly haunted now, became

unendurable. I got up off the bed and went back to the living-room. Lucia was vacuuming over by the window.

"I'm going out."

She switched off the vacuum. "What you say, Mr. Duluth?"

"I'm going out."

"Okay. And don't you go breaking your heart now. It'll all be all right."

"Goodbye, Lucia."

I didn't feel up to going to the office and exposing myself to the sage advice and the sympathy of Miss Mills. I walked at random to Third Avenue. Sunlight was splashing down through the El. Trucks lumbered by. People were walking back and forth past the little delicatessens and the cluttered windows of the antique stores. I turned south. I could extract no nourishment from the bustle around me. It was as if Third Avenue rejected me, as if everyone who hurried by could see that I was walking hand in hand with a ghost.

I came to a movie house and went in. Next to sleep, movies are the best anodyne. But Nanny Ordway was still with me. I could almost feel her in the empty seat next to me. If I shifted my knee one inch to the left, it would touch hers. If I turned my head, there she would be with her dark hair flopping around her shoulders, her pale, little-girl face tilted upward as she watched the figures on the screen.

She was with me after the movies when I went out into the sunlight again. She followed me to the Riker's where I ate because I had to eat something. I walked up to Central Park and wandered around. I tried a big, brassy stage show at the Roxy, but I couldn't shake Nanny Ordway.

When I returned to the apartment at six o'clock, she

came too. She was sitting on the window seat, looking down at the East River. *It's lovely—the room—the window. What nonsense I talked about being poor!*

She had taken Iris' place and moved in.

I had a couple of martinis. I was a little wary of drink, so I went into the kitchen, found a can of soup, heated it, and drank it. I ate some cheese and crackers too. I knew then that Nanny Ordway had me on the run. The only thing to do was to turn and fight. Knowledge is power. Francis Bacon had said that and presumably he knew what he was talking about. The only way to defeat Nanny Ordway was to obtain more knowledge of her.

If, for example, I could find someone who had known her, who could prove that she had been mad, then I could take that person to Iris and even to Lieutenant Trant. But where could I start my search? Incredible as it now sounded, I knew virtually nothing about Nanny Ordway. Once she had mentioned a mother, but the publicized fact of her death had, apparently, caused no relative or friend to come forward. It was as if she had deliberately fostered her anonymity.

There was only one person who could help me. Miss Amberley.

I made myself another martini. I would need it if I had to face Miss Amberley. There was no use phoning and finding out whether she was in. If she knew I was coming, she'd barricade the door. I'd have to go down there and somehow force myself on her.

I drank the martini. The phone rang. I rushed to answer it. I suppose I thought it would be Iris. It was Miss Mills.

"Hello, Peter."

"Hello."

"Iris just called me."

"She did?"

"She told me everything, about the letter and all. She's very unhappy."

"I know."

"I tried to argue with her but there wasn't anything I could do. Peter, you can't blame her."

"Of course not."

"I suppose I ought to be bright and cheerful and full of cosy little prospects for the future. But we're neither of us quite that moronic, are we?"

"No."

"Peter, are you all right?"

"I'm all right."

"Don't come to the office tomorrow if you don't feel like it. My weary old shoulders can carry it for a while. But if there's any room in your life for a pig-lady, God-damit, Peter, you know I'd do anything."

"Thanks, Miss Mills."

"And there's one thing more I think you should know. That policeman, Lieutenant Trant, was around this afternoon. He asked a lot of questions—exactly when you came in from that movie, whether I could find any more of the drawings Nanny made, things like that. I was a little worried. I thought you said the case was closed so far as homicide was concerned."

"That's what I thought."

"Well, it isn't."

That was a comforting piece of news!

"He's a charmer, that one. He turned on the full male heat—special brand reserved for older girls. He could tell how smart I was, how I would be the first to realize that it was best for everyone's sake to have the truth established. All that crap. He was smooth, too—didn't give away a darn thing. Peter, do you want me to try to find out what he's up to?"

"Think you can?"

"Oh, sure, I put on the greatest seduced act since Madame Butterfly. He thinks I'm mad for him. He told me if ever I thought of anything, any little thing, I was to run around to his office at the station-house. Then I'll try it? I'll go around and snuff about tomorrow?"

"Fine."

Miss Mills did not speak for a moment, but the line was still active.

"Peter, it was right to tell you that, wasn't it?"

"Of course it was." I knew she was miserable because she, like Lottie, was wondering whether or not I'd break. I didn't want her to be miserable. I had caused enough trouble already. I said: "Don't worry about me."

"Worry? Me worry? Don't be silly, Peter. Gay as a lark, I."

She hung up. Now that I had heard about Lieutenant Trant, I was glad I'd had that third martini. I went out and took a taxi to 31 Charlton Street.

CHAPTER THIRTEEN

The taxi driver lost his way. Drivers often do in the Village. They're used to the geometric simplicity of Uptown Manhattan. A few inconsistencies, a twist or two in a street and they are defeated. We came to Charlton Street from the wrong direction past gloomy, night-closed factories which gave the impression of life vegetated.

I couldn't get Lieutenant Trant out of my mind. Had the final autopsy reports come in and, incredibly, pointed to murder? I doubted it. Only yesterday Trant had said they would take several days. Was then his moral indignation against me so extreme that for some private satisfaction of his own, he was jumping the gun and starting a murder investigation anyway? I doubted that, too. Detectives—even detectives like Lieutenant Trant —didn't operate that way.

If he was starting an investigation, it was because he had found some other evidence to believe that Nanny Ordway might have been murdered. Something, perhaps, connected with the drawings he had mentioned to Miss Mills.

A new idea that chilled came to me. Could Nanny have intended exactly this? Could she have been monstrous enough to have wanted her dream lover not only to lose his wife and his self-respect but also to be accused of her death? The secret of love merged with the secret of death? Why not? And why shouldn't she succeed? She'd succeeded at everything else.

For certainly it was I and only I whom Lieutenant Trant would suspect. I remembered what I had thought of him at the station-house—that, if he believed I was guilty of any crime punishable by law, he would track me to the ends of the earth. *"I'd start by checking your alibi."* That was what he had said. And that, almost certainly, was what he had done before he had gone to Miss Mills. It was not probable that anyone would have recognized me at the movie house. Why should they?

Suddenly I saw myself hopelessly caught in a dead girl's dream. I saw myself with two Furies stalking me now, Nanny Ordway and her dupe Lieutenant Trant—the "Victim" and the Law. I saw myself running a race against time—to prove Nanny Ordway's insanity before that insanity destroyed me.

The entrance to Number 31 was below street level. I went down the stone steps and pressed the buzzer marked Claire Amberley. Nanny's name wasn't written on the dog-eared card. Had Miss Amberley removed it already? Or had it never been there? I couldn't remember.

An answering buzz sounded in the closed front door. I pushed it inward and walked up the chocolate-painted staircase to the second floor. As I turned from the stairhead into the landing, Miss Amberley was hovering outside her half-open door. She was wearing a green, paint-stained smock. I hadn't known that artists or anyone else for that matter wore smocks any more. It stopped just below her knees, making her look even gawkier than I had remembered her. I hadn't expected to come upon her so suddenly. She obviously had not expected me either. A flush spread over her face. It was an unbecoming, spinsterish flush which belonged with a much older woman.

"You!" she said. "What are you doing here?"

I thought irrelevantly that here was another cliché that

I must remember next time I directed a play. Clichés were beginning to pile up on me. I said, "I want to talk to you."

"Well, you can't. Not possibly."

She took a step backward, fluttery and frightened, as if I were about to rape her. In so big, so mannish a girl, it was absurd, annoying, and somehow pathetic.

"My brother's here. He's just arrived from Wood's Hole. He . . ."

Her banal social apologies petered out. She put her hand on the door. I had the impression that at any second she was going to bolt into the apartment. Then the door was pushed open from inside and a young man came out.

"What is it, Claire?"

Miss Amberley swung around. "John, it's—Mr. Duluth." She spoke my name as if it were Jack the Ripper.

The young man was tall and thin with a small head on a long neck. He had a short crew hair-cut and a stiff, university manner. His nondescript face was just saved from being homely by a pair of steady, intelligent blue eyes. He looked tired or sick.

He said, "I'm John Amberley, Claire's brother. What do you want, Mr. Duluth?"

"I want to talk to your sister."

"No." Now that she had a man to protect her, Miss Amberley wasn't frightened any more, and her face had taken on the expression of spite and revulsion which I remembered from Lieutenant Trant's office. "I refuse to talk to him, John."

Her brother put his hand on her arm. "What do you want to talk about, Mr. Duluth?"

"Nanny Ordway," I said.

"No," said Miss Amberley again. "No."

For a moment her brother hesitated. Then he said, "Come in, Mr. Duluth."

"John!" cried Miss Amberley.

"Please, Claire. I want to talk to him. It can't make things any worse than they are."

Miss Amberley was surprisingly biddable. She didn't object any more, and let him guide her inside the apartment. I followed.

The room with the navy blue walls was even more cluttered than I had remembered. The easel had been dragged into the middle of the floor. One of the gray and brown Braqueish still-life, half finished, was standing on it. I had expected to feel Nanny Ordway here even more violently than in my own apartment. But I had been wrong. The books scattered on the studio couches, the wilting violets in a cheese glass, the highbrow disarray struck no responsive chord. It all fitted exactly with Miss Amberley. This was obviously her atmosphere. Nanny Ordway had merely been an interloper.

Claire Amberley moved to the easel and stood beside it, rejecting me with every ounce of her being. Her brother said, "Sit down, Mr. Duluth."

He pushed some books aside on one of the studio couches and sat down himself, arranging his long, bony legs. I sat on the other couch. He couldn't have been much more than thirty, but, as with his sister, there was an elderly air to him. I thought he was probably a master at one of the more elegant boy's prep schools. He had that manner, the carefully underplayed dignity of an adult accustomed to the society of adolescents.

"Just what do you want to know about Nanny Ordway, Mr. Duluth?"

"As much as I can."

"Why?"

"Because she was found dead in my apartment. Because, according to your sister, I had promised to marry her when, in fact, I hardly knew her. Because she's managed to make a superlative mess of my life. Isn't that reason enough to be curious?"

"A mess of *his* life!" cried Miss Amberley. "Did you hear that, John? What did I tell you?"

John Amberley put his hands on his knees. He was watching me with an odd intentness as if every detail of my appearance had some private importance for him.

"This isn't an easy situation, Mr. Duluth."

"Did anyone say it was?"

"No. But it's a little more complicated than you may realize." He paused. "You see, I was in love with Nanny Ordway. I had asked her to be my wife."

He made that unexpected announcement quietly, almost diffidently. It took me completely by surprise, and I felt a kind of weary despair. I had come here in the hopes of proving Nanny Ordway had been insane. All I found was a man who had asked her to marry him!

Suddenly I felt once again Nanny Ordway's immediate physical presence, as if her dead hand was in mine. No. Not her hand. That was wrong. Because now I thought of her as a spider, a gray, unobtrusive little spider spinning delicate, devious webs, crouching in dark corners, crouching only to spring down the threads at her victims. The "Victim's" victims. Me . . . John Amberley . . . Who else?

I said with disgust, "Is there no end to this thing?"

"She's dead," said John Amberley softly. "That's some kind of an end, isn't it?"

"I suppose you're like your sister. You think I'm responsible."

"Does it matter what I think?"

"Of course it matters. Would you like to be branded

by all and sundry as a seducer? Would you like to go around bellowing the truth at the top of your lungs and have no one pay the slightest attention?"

"Why should anyone pay attention?" It was Miss Amberley's cold, cutting voice that broke in. "There's nothing hard to understand about you. In the beginning you were too craven to accept the moral guilt of having killed her. Now you're stuck with your story and you can't break down. How would you look if you did, if you admitted you were a cowardly liar as well as a corrupter of young girls?"

There it was—the same old argument against me. It was what they all believed. It was what even Iris believed. There was no point in wearing myself out in futile battles with Miss Amberley. I turned back to her brother.

"When did all this happen?"

"I asked Nanny to marry me a few weeks ago. On my birthday, as a matter of fact."

"And she accepted?" I wouldn't have been surprised if she had. Nothing about Nanny Ordway could surprise me any more.

"She neither accepted nor refused, Mr. Duluth. She asked me to wait a while."

"Why?"

"Because of you, of course," put in Miss Amberley. "She was still hoping you'd divorce your wife, that you wouldn't let her down."

I ignored her. "Is that the reason she gave you, Mr. Amberley?"

"She gave no reason. I didn't press her."

"But I *did.*" Miss Amberley wasn't to be ignored. She flounced into the conversation again, her arms folded across the front of her floppy smock. The pose gave her a pseudo-oriental caste. She looked ludicrous, like a Wellesley girl playing a mandarin in a Drama Group production of a No play. But there was nothing ludicrous about the malice in her voice and in the protuberant green eyes. "That's when I made her confide in me, the day she'd told John to wait. I knew there was another man. I'd suspected it for some time. I urged, I begged, I pleaded for John's sake. Finally she told me about you. She admitted she was in love with the husband of a famous actress. Oh, she was loyal to you, of course. Nanny was always loyal. But it all came out when you called—the whole, charming, sweet-smelling story that I told to Lieutenant Trant."

It would have been less horrible if she had not been enjoying herself so much. She was just like Lottie. There must be something about my predicament, I thought, that gave women a sexual titillation. Nanny Ordway had me, like a prisoner of the Arabs, tied to a bench for the women to mutilate. Miss Amberley was having a wonderful time with her knife.

I glanced at her, too bored with her to feel any antagonism. "Did you tell Lieutenant Trant about your brother's involvement in this?"

"I certainly did not."

"Why?"

"Hadn't you done enough damage already? Did my brother's name have to get splashed all over the headlines? He's a responsible man with a responsible job. Does he have to be martyrized too?"

All those rhetorical questions! John Amberley was still sitting there quietly on the couch with the piles of books pushing against his thin hips. He was obviously suffering. I understood that tired, sick, look now—it was the look of a man who had tragically lost his girl. I was very nearly exhausted. I thought: What's the use of going on? Is it worth tormenting him and myself—for what? I'll never prove anything here. But something, maybe the fading support of the martinis, made me persist.

I said, "Mr. Amberley, did Nanny Ordway tell you all these lies about me too?"

"She never mentioned your name. I never realized . . . That is, until I read in the papers, until I came here this evening and Claire told me . . ."

"I'd kept it from him," cut in Miss Amberley. "He loved her. Why should I have made him unhappy with all that filth?"

"You didn't think it'd make him unhappy to marry her—even though you thought she was having an affair with another man?"

Miss Amberley flushed. "I was trying to save Nanny. You wouldn't understand that. If she'd married John, she would have been saved."

Dear little Nanny Ordway who'd had to be saved from me. "Okay, okay," I said. I turned back to John Amberley. "She was mad."

"Mad!" shrilled Miss Amberley. "How dare you suggest . . . !"

"She was mad," I persisted. "Can I possibly make you believe that, Mr. Amberley? Nanny Ordway was insane."

John Amberley's face was white. In a thin, closed voice, he asked, "You expect me to believe that a girl with whom I was in love could have been insane without my realizing it?"

"She fooled you. The way she fooled me and your sister."

"That's a lie," cried Miss Amberley. "A filthy, disgusting lie."

"Yes," said John Amberley very quietly, "that is a lie, Mr. Duluth."

His restraint, his underemphasized contempt were

much more deadly than his sister's bald hostility. It was hopeless. It was trying to prove black was white again.

I said, "I'm sorry for you. Do you at least believe that?"

"Oh, yes. You probably are. I am sorry for myself." Surprisingly the ghost of a smile haunted his lips. "I'm learning quite a lot of things about myself, Mr. Duluth. None of them are very attractive. I'm a meteorologist by profession, you know. It's my job to sift a mass of frequently conflicting data, to correlate it and to reach some satisfactory conclusion. In the laboratory, even the most complex problems sooner or later succumb to the scientific method. One of the things I've discovered about myself is that I can't import that scientific method into my private life. It should be possible to admit that you may believe what you say, that there was some mistake with Nanny, that you are not what I think you are. But I can't keep an open mind. I can't. I can only sit here and look at you and think . . ."

He brought a clenched fist up to his mouth. It was a little child's gesture. I'd seen babies do it to try to keep themselves from crying. It was a shocking, naked moment.

I got up. "You shouldn't have let me in."

"No. I'm sorry. Please. Don't go." Anger at himself or shame had given him control again. "If I feel a shabby emotion, I don't have to give way to it. You have your problems too. You came here to ask questions. If it can help you . . . If anyone can be helped, it's better than this. Go ahead. Ask whatever you like."

He was a very strange young man. I sat down again. Oddly enough, I was staying now for his sake as much as for my own.

"All right," I said. "Can you tell me the name of anyone else who knew her—anyone who might still have an open mind about her?"

The faint smile still lingered on his lips as if he thought I had used his phrase "an open mind" to mock him and approved of my mockery.

"I'm afraid I can't help you there, Mr. Duluth. Nanny came into our life by chance. We knew nothing of her friends."

"What about her parents?"

"They are both dead. They came from Virginia. Quite a good old family, apparently, but they were poor. They were both killed in an automobile accident when she was sixteen. Since then she had been on her own."

"She talked once as if her mother were still alive."

"Well, she isn't," snapped Miss Amberley, cutting off that channel.

I went on, "How long have you known her, Mr. Amberley?"

"About six months."

"Where did you meet her?"

"Here in the Village. At a nightclub." John Amberley glanced at his sister. "What was its name, Claire?"

"What difference does it make?"

"Oh, yes, Sylvia's. On West Tenth Street. She was working there as a waitress."

"A waitress?"

"They have girls waiting on table," said John Amberley. "It's all very informal. One of those carefree, Bohemian places. I was down from Wood's Hole for the week-end. Claire took me there. It's one of her haunts. I don't have much experience with what you might call night-life. She thought it might amuse me. Nanny happened to be the waitress who served us. She—she was obviously different from the other girls, more intelligent, more sensitive. There was some fool thing about Henry James. I had *The Ambassadors* with me. She made some remark about it. I didn't expect a waitress in a nightclub to know about Henry James. But he was her favorite author. After she'd brought out beer, she sat down at the table with us. That's allowed at the club. It's that sort of place. We got to talking. And both Claire and I . . . Didn't we, Claire?"

He broke off. He looked vague, as if he had lost track of what he had been going to say. I realized then just how much of an effort it was for him to talk this way and marveled at the self-discipline that impelled him, against every inclination, to help a man who—so far as he knew—had caused his girl's suicide.

But my interest in him was overshadowed by my absorption in Nanny Ordway. For the first time, I was seeing her doing things that had not been connected with me, leading the life which, in the end, had caused such havoc for all of us. I could see her vividly in that arty Village nightclub, aggressively unobtrusive, quiet-spoken, with her hair flopping over her face, young, naïve, getting the subtle effect.

Henry James. Oh, excuse me for mentioning it, but I'm mad about Henry James.

Claire Amberley had crossed to her brother's side. She stood with her hand on his shoulder like a clumsy, militant muse.

"John, don't talk any more. Why should you torture yourself for him?"

"Please, Claire, let me do this my way. Mr. Duluth, does this give any picture? Does this help?"

"Help!" snorted Miss Amberley.

I said, "I'd be very grateful if you'd go on."

"Well, she sat there with us, off and on, when she wasn't serving, all evening. We talked about lots of things. She was so quick, so alive. Both Claire and I were impressed. We went back the next evening, didn't we, Claire? And that time she told us something of

134

herself. She was living in some furnished room with another girl."

"What girl?"

"Oh, I don't know that. She didn't say. But it was all very inconvenient for her and—well, before the evening was out, Claire suggested she should move in here with her. Nanny was terribly diffident. She always hated accepting favors. But between us, we managed to persuade her."

The way I had managed to persuade her to take my key! I could see Nanny Ordway again in Claire Amberley's blue satin evening dress (had she had to be persuaded into borrowing that too?), turning quickly from the window seat while I held the key out to her. *Oh, no, no, I could never* . . . Nanny Ordway who hated accepting favors but who always seemed to have ended up accepting them. A furnished room with an unknown girl—Miss Amberley and the Village—me and Sutton Place. Always a step up. There was a character clue that was all too sane.

John Amberley's voice was running on. "I had to go back to Wood's Hole after the week-end, of course, but Nanny moved in with Claire the next day. Both Claire and I had decided that there was no point in her going on working at that place. It wasn't right for her. And she'd told us how it was her dream to be a writer. . . . Well, Claire was perfectly prepared to let her live in the apartment with her as long as she liked, to give her a chance with her writing. She was company for Claire and . . ."

"And she was mad, of course," put in Miss Amberley's voice, gravid with sarcasm. "Naturally when I picked a girl to live with me, to be my friend, I would choose a raving maniac."

John Amberley was saying, "I came down again the

next week-end. The three of us went about together. Claire had got very fond of her then. And I—well, I've never been particularly a ladies' man, Mr. Duluth. I've always been absorbed with my work and . . . and, well, a bit shy maybe. But with Nanny it was different. She wasn't one of those girls who make you feel small. She . . . I started to write to her and she wrote back. I came down whenever I could. She seemed to be fond of me, at least as Claire's brother, and she was interested in the family. We've been in Boston a good many generations, you know. There are quite a lot of interesting ancestors. Of course, we don't have as much money as we used to. But I knew things like that didn't matter to her. I knew she was sweet and fine, much too good for me. I should have guessed she would have far—far more stimulating, glamorous men interested in her. But I didn't realize. I—I thought I had a chance. I asked her to marry me. And—well, that's all, really."

His naïve frankness and his humility were embarrassing now. I understood him even less than I had. Perhaps there was some New England guilt sense that urged him on to strip himself bare in front of me as an atonement for hating me as a "successful" rival.

He made a little gesture with his hand toward his sister. "Perhaps, Mr. Duluth, there's something else you would like to ask Claire?"

"I don't think there is," said Miss Amberley. "I think he's had enough of me already." She was the Arab woman with the knife again. "Would you like to hear any more, Mr. Duluth? Would you like to hear her pitiful confessions of love? Her anxieties about the divorce? Her trust, her touching faith in your sincerity? Her hopes that you weren't just using her, that you would stand by your promises, that it would come out right in the end? Would you like to hear what she thought of my brother? How much she respected him? How much she would have liked to settle down quietly with him and marry him—but how one part of her was spell-bound by you? Oh, that's only a beginning. I could talk indefinitely. I could give you countless examples of her screaming insanity."

Miss Amberley was right. I'd had enough of her. I got up. I said, "I'm sure you could talk indefinitely, Miss Amberley, but I think that's a pleasure I'll forego." I crossed to John Amberley. I held out my hand. "Thanks. You've been very kind."

He looked at my hand a moment and then took it. "I'm sorry, Mr. Duluth. I should have been able to control myself a great deal better."

Suddenly Miss Amberley laughed. "Listen to them. Isn't it wonderful? The two noble males kissing and making up!"

The green protuberant eyes fixed me then with a look of undiluted malevolence.

"What does it feel like to be such a charmer? To meet you is to love you, isn't it? Everyone falls at your feet."

"Yes," I said savagely, "the nation's sweetheart. That's me."

"But it's too bad, isn't it, that people see through you in the end?" Her tongue came out to moisten her lips. It was a mannerism I remembered from the station-house. Dimly I wondered whether that was why she didn't wear lipstick—because she was tired of the taste of it.

"Yes," she said. "Take your wife, for example."

"What about my wife?"

"Oh, nothing." She shrugged. "Just that she was here this afternoon. She's charming, perfectly charming. Poor dear, it was really pathetic. She so much wanted to believe your extraordinary theory that Nanny was mad.

She even had some gullible idea that I would back you up. But once I'd told her about John, about what a wonderful person Nanny really was, she realized, of course, just how gullible the idea had been. She left here, I assure you, fully informed and with no illusions."

She crossed to the door and opened it for me. I thought how delighted she was going to be when Lieutenant Trant showed up one fine morning and announced that I was a murderer as well as a moral leper. She wouldn't be able to contain herself for joy.

"Yes, Mr. Duluth." She was still smiling. This was to be the final, orgiastic thrust of the knife. "I'm afraid you don't have a wife any more. Too bad, isn't it? Drop in again whenever you're in the neighborhood. I'm almost always here."

CHAPTER FOURTEEN

I walked out onto Charlton Street. A mist had come up from the river. It impregnated the air with dampness and blurred the street lights. Claire Amberley's final announcement had hurt me just as much as it had been intended to hurt. I might have guessed Iris would visit her. In her confusion and unhappiness, who else was there to whom she could turn for enlightenment? Like me, she had hoped that Miss Amberley might somehow hold out a lifeline. Well, she knew better now.

I struggled against a desire to call my wife. Even before Miss Amberley, a call could have got us nowhere. It was doubly hopeless now. Miss Amberley, large, pink-faced, triumphant, still loomed in my mind. Damn her, I thought, damn her for a meddling, evil-minded bitch. But it was stupid to blame her—just as it had been stupid to imagine I could glean any help from her. Claire Amberley, in her starved, man-shy way, had been as enamored of Nanny Ordway as her brother. She wasn't a real villain. She was only another victim.

It was Nanny Ordway from whom all horror flowed and who still, even after the halting confessions of John Amberley, remained remorselessly enigmatic. Nanny Ordway, whom I had seen as a spider but who now seemed to me like this mist, intangible, insidious, stealing tentacle-wise through my clothes, crawling even down my throat into my lungs.

I turned out of Charlton Street into Sixth Avenue. I

saw a bar and went into it, bringing trails of mist with me. A couple of customers sat on stools drearily watching vaudeville on a television set. I ordered a rye and water. I didn't have any faith in its effect, but it might at least cloud out the Amberleys.

All it did was to make me think of Lieutenant Trant. Would he show up at the apartment tomorrow, maybe, and accuse me of murder? If he did, what could I say in my own defense which hadn't already been said a dozen times?

Nothing.

There was still Sylvia's on West Tenth Street—the only doorway left open that might lead me to the real Nanny Ordway.

Sylvia's. That was all.

On television some disinterred comic was singing "*If you knew Susie*" and making like Eddie Cantor. I paid for my drink and went out into the mist, looking for a taxi to take me to Sylvia's.

I found a taxi and the driver found Sylvia's, grumbling at the mist, grumbling at the lot of all taxi drivers, but surprisingly picking out Sylvia's from a warren of other, obscure little nightclubs.

The place was in darkness. I told the driver to wait and went to try the door. It was locked. I stood a moment glowering at the darkened door, feeling that even glass and metal and wood had turned against me.

But there was nothing I could do. I knew the end of a day when I saw one. I got back into the taxi and gave my home address. Nanny Ordway climbed into the taxi with me. She was still there when I got out at Sutton Place.

She went to bed with me that night, too.

I was awakened next morning by the front door buzzer. My first thought, bringing a cold flutter in my stomach, was: Lieutenant Trant. I went to the door in my pajamas. Brian was standing there. He looked very handsome and unhappy.

"Hi, Peter, can I come in?"

"Sure."

He walked into the living-room. "I can't stay. Lottie doesn't know I'm here. I told her I was going around the block for cigarettes. Peter, you had a big fight with her yesterday."

Had I? "Yes," I said. "That's right."

"She's terribly mad."

"I wouldn't doubt it."

"She's really on the rampage. Last night at the theater and then again this morning. Peter, I hate to butt in, but you'd better come up and try to calm her down."

The mere thought of Lottie made me tired. "I'm sorry, Brian. I can't face her right now."

"You'd better. She's going to break her contract."

"She can't break her contract."

"There's a sickness clause."

"But she's not sick."

"Lottie can be anything she wants to be. You know that. She's worked herself up into the tizzy of all time. She's babbling about her heart, her nerves. She's going to call Doctor Norris. She's going to make him write a certificate saying she has to have two weeks off for her nerves. I can't do anything with her. Maybe you can't either any more. But, for your own sake, you'd better try."

So here it was. Nanny Ordway was still on the job. Without Lottie, *Star Rising* automatically shut down. Without Lottie, I'd have the whole production on full pay on my hands without a penny coming in. Probably, too, I would have the play die under me if Lottie chose to go on being "nervous" indefinitely.

At any other time, this would have been a major tragedy to be averted at all costs. But I, who had lost so much, still had my pride, and now my pride was more important than my pocket-book. I was damned if I was going to eat any more mud, go crawling up there begging Lottie Marin to forgive me because she'd accused me of every sin in the calendar and tried to break up my marriage.

Brian was watching me hopefully.

I said, "Thanks for letting me know. But I couldn't be less impressed. If she's that much of a bastard, let her go ahead and do whatever she wants to do."

"But you know Lottie, Peter. She doesn't really mean it. She just gets worked up."

"Yes," I said, "she's a charmer and thank God you're the one that's married to her and not me."

"Then you won't try?"

"I won't."

He stood a moment in silence. "Okay. I see your point. I don't blame you." He paused. "Has Iris really moved out?"

"She has."

"She shouldn't have done that."

"She's done it."

"Where is she?"

"I don't want Lottie to know. She's done enough damage already."

"I wish you'd tell me. I wouldn't tell Lottie."

"Why do you want to know?"

He flushed. "I just thought—maybe I'd go talk to her. Hell, do you think I feel good about it all? Lottie barging in and everything?"

"You wouldn't get anywhere."

"I don't know. Maybe I could straighten her out.

Peter, let me try. I'd feel a lot better. And I won't tell Lottie—honest."

He looked at me pleadingly as if he was asking me to do him a favor instead of wanting to do one for me. It was nice to have a friend.

"Okay," I said.

I gave him the address of Iris' hotel. He grinned.

"Fine. I'll try to make her see sense. Well, I'd better be running along or I'll catch hell." He started for the door and then turned. "Sure you won't come up and try?"

"Quite sure."

"Okay. You know best. Bye, now."

After Miss Amberley, I hadn't any hopes of Brian as an ambassador to Iris, but his kindness in offering himself made me feel a little better about Lottie's betrayal. I went into the kitchen and made some coffee. I was drinking it when the phone rang. It was Miss Mills.

"Morning, Peter. How are you?"

"Alive. Anything more from Trant?"

"Not yet. Do you still want me to go around to the station-house and try him out?"

"Yes."

"Fine. Listen, I'm weaseling on my promise. I said I'd hold the office down without you. But I can't. Thomas Wood's here."

Thomas Wood was the author of *Let Live*.

"He's just flown in bright as a bird from Ann Arbor, clapping his wings, full of fun and scholarly wit. He thought he'd surprise us, he said."

"That's nice."

"Peter, he's bursting with plans for the play and raring to meet a real live producer. I'm not important enough. He has me tabbed as an old mop you keep around to wipe the floor with. I'm sorry, but you've just got to come and cope."

"All right," I said. "Have you heard about Lottie?"

"What about the darling thing?"

"She's going to be sick. Yesterday I called her a couple of well-chosen names. Now she's getting Doctor Norris to write out a certificate for a two weeks' release from the play. Nervous exhaustion."

"Peter, you can't let her do that. Go right upstairs and whimper like a cocker spaniel."

"I'd rather choke to death."

She paused and then said resignedly, "Okay, if that's the way the land lies. Want me to try?"

"Can you see it working?"

"No, frankly. Then there'll be no performance this afternoon?"

"Not if she goes through with it."

"Shall I notify the cast?"

"Better wait till we hear officially."

"Well, well," said Miss Mills, "what a lovely week we're having. Your Taurus must be in a particularly dreary trine. Listen, you've simply got to come and charm Mr. Wood now. We don't want to lose two plays in one fell et cetera."

"That's right."

"Then the moment you show up, I'll go around to Trant."

I went to the office. Miss Mills had already called Trant with some cock-and-bull story of wanting his advice. He'd said to come right around. She kissed me.

"Peter, I don't look too much like a spy, do I?"

"No."

"Well, I'll do my best. You do your best with Mr. Wood. He's in your office."

Dramatists who have just had their first play accepted

fall into one of two categories. Either they are little mice who don't dare say boo to an assistant stage manager or else they're George Bernard Shaw. Thomas Wood was George Bernard Shaw. He wanted tickets for all the hit shows. He wanted interviews. Even though the play had hardly got off my desk, he was full of inspirations for direction, casting and sets. To make it worse, in his professorial Michigan retreat he didn't seem to read the lurid newspapers. His greatest inspiration was that the chief female part in *Let Live* was a natural for Iris. As a matter of fact, it would have suited her, but I spent an uncomfortable period giving him every reason but the right one as to why I didn't think she would consider it. I suppose I could have told him the truth—that my wife had left me because a girl had been found hanging from my bedroom chandelier.

It was over an hour before I finally got rid of him, and even then I had to promise to get him matinee tickets and to take him to dinner and another show myself that evening. He expected it and I couldn't afford to antagonize him.

Just after he left the office, Lottie's agent called. He had never liked me and he got quite a kick out of announcing Lottie's "nervous collapse." I fumed and fretted for the book, but I knew there was nothing I could do. Dr. Norris, of course, had given his certificate. I could just see him, brisk, cheerful, thrilled to death at doing a favor for a Star. The agent offered to bring the certificate around so that I could frame it and hang it on the wall. I slammed down the receiver. The stenographer started trying to contact the cast. I went around to the theater to get the announcement of a two week shut-down posted.

The stage manager happened to be there. I told him to put up a notice on the bulletin board. While we were talking, Gordon Ling came out of his dressing-room. Gordon was one of those small-time actors who always hang around the theater when they're working, probably because they're bored with their dreary little furnished rooms and the theater makes them feel they're big-shots.

"Lottie's not really sick, is she?"

"That's what her doctor says."

His handsomely aging face broke into an awkward smile. "You're having a rough time, Peter."

"We take the rough with the smooth."

"She was bitchy last night. You should have heard her."

"I'm sure it was a liberal education."

"Peter, I wish there was something I could do." I was surprised, looking at him, to realize that he meant it. I'd never thought Gordon Ling had any feeling for me. When you're down, you find sympathy in the most unexpected places. "How about lunch on me? Think that would do any good?"

"Well . . ." I began.

Then Iris' voice broke in behind me. "Sorry, Gordon, but Peter's having lunch with me."

I turned. My wife was standing just inside the stage door in front of the Bulletin Board. She was smiling. But it wasn't a real smile; it was something she was putting on for Gordon, the stage door man, and whoever else happened to be around—a public smile.

"That's all right, isn't it, Peter?"

"Sure."

"They told me at the office that you were here."

She took my arm. We went out together into the alley that led to the street. Her arrival had taken me completely by surprise. I felt very shy and tense.

She said awkwardly, "This is Brian's idea."

So that was it.

"He came around. He was very sweet. He said why not have lunch with Peter, at least? It'll look better for the columnists if nothing else. Go somewhere where you'll be seen, like Sardi's. Shall we go to Sardi's?"

"Okay," I said. My voice was just as awkward as hers.

Sardi's was just around the corner. We went there and were given our usual table. A lot of theatrical people were eating lunch. They all looked at us. From the point of view of Brian's plan for concealing the fact that we had split up, their polite curiosity helped. But it didn't help us as man and wife. It was the goldfish treatment plus.

I knew, almost at once, that it was going to be the most disastrous lunch of my life because Iris was trying to hate me. She didn't hate me yet. I knew that. If she had, she wouldn't have come to lunch just because Brian had asked her to. But she was trying. Nanny's letter had poisoned her; Miss Amberley had poisoned her. She'd had plenty of time to think in her hotel bedroom, and there was only one conclusion she could have reached —that I was a louse. That was why she was fighting against me and against her love for me.

Over cocktails, I said: "I hear you were at Miss Amberley's yesterday afternoon?"

"Yes."

"She made it worse, didn't she?"

Iris carefully did not look at me. "She told me about her brother."

"Whose beautiful romance I blighted."

She flared suddenly: "Is that so funny? That a man was in love with her and wanted to marry her? That, in spite of all that, you . . ."

"I—what?"

She did look at me then. "Peter, if only you'd told

me the truth from the beginning. . . . If only you'd trusted me, instead of lying, evading. . . ."

I felt a kind of savage mirth. If I'd trusted her! If I'd admitted that I'd been a fool, a seducer and a knave—she would have forgiven me! Everything would have been dandy!

The injustice of it all was too much for me and I said bitterly, "You and Lottie."

Her eyes glinted. "And what does that mean? Me and Lottie?"

"You're just the same. There's not a cent's worth of difference between you."

"What a thing to say!"

"It's true. It . . ." The futility of my anger occurred to me. "Iris, baby, I'm sorry."

"Please!"

"I've missed you so much."

"No, Peter. No."

After that we talked a little, but it was practically impossible to think of subjects without overtones. I didn't mention that Lieutenant Trant would probably arrest me at any minute; I didn't even mention Lottie's secession. I was afraid, if I did, she would imagine I was trying to make her sorry for me. Every moment was torture now, but I was already dreading the time when it would have to be over.

We dragged it out somehow until coffee. Then Alec Ryder came over from another table. It was almost a relief to see him. As usual, he treated us exactly as if we were just another married couple of whom he was fond.

"I seem to be giving a party tonight. I do hope you'll both come."

I said, "I'm sorry. I've got a playwright on my hands."

He turned to Iris, smooth as his Bronzini silk tie. "How about you, Iris? You can make it, can't you?"

Iris glanced at me quickly, then she looked back at Alec. "Yes," she said, "I think I can. Yes, Alec, I'd love it."

"Fine. Around six-thirty."

He went back to his table. A faint flush was spreading over my wife's cheeks. I could read her thoughts as clearly as if they were scrawled across the menu. She was going to take up Alec's offer to do the play in England.

"Iris . . ." I began.

Her bright smile chilled off my words. "It's getting rather late. I really think I should be leaving."

Late for what? Leaving to go where? I looked at her. I thought in total defeat: Is this the last time I'm ever going to see her?

"All right," I said. "I'll get the check."

CHAPTER FIFTEEN

She got up quickly and left the table before the waiter came. A lot of people watched her taut, hurried flight toward the door. She' hadn't, I knew, meant to expose our marital quandary to the world. She'd left because the tension between us had become as unendurable for her as for me. But the damage was done. Brian's well-intended scheme had boomeranged. All afternoon theatrical telephones would be jangling.

"My dear, have you heard the latest Nanny Ordway thing? Peter and Iris were at Sardi's for lunch and . . ."

Alec Ryder and his party, passing the table on their way out, gave me careful smiles. The waiter came with the check.

I said, "Get me a double brandy."

He brought it. I gulped most of it and ordered a second. I knew I was giving up. The moment of ultimate blackness which I had, half resignedly, been awaiting from the beginning had finally arrived. Now it had come, it brought with it an almost voluptuous sense of relief. I'd fought. I'd done my best. I'd lost. Okay. Let Nanny Ordway have her full triumph—with half of Sardi's looking on.

I had almost finished the second drink and was sitting with the glass tilted in my hand when a strange sensation began to stir in me. It was a peculiar feeling of recognition as if the tilted brandy glass, my own knuckles bent around it, even the wrinkled tablecloth all had some immense significance which was just beyond my grasp. It had happened before. All this had happened before. In some nightmare, in some . . .

It came to me then. Of course! Twelve years ago—the night after my first wife died! I had been sitting just here—at this same table. *A double brandy.* I could hear my own voice from the past as I gave the order. I could even see the waiter. Not the same waiter who had served Iris and me today, but another one who had left years ago. Luigi. That had been his name. Luigi, with his tired waiter's smile and his big, hairy wrists sticking out of his waiter's jacket.

That had been the beginning. *A double brandy*—and this sensation of relief, this perverse pleasure in yielding. Let it all go. Who cares?

Suddenly I was plunged back into the sordid months of collapse that had followed, months stale with self-pity and the smell of alcohol, spiraling downward to their nadir in the discreet, expensive sanitarium. Had I learnt nothing from all that? Did I have to go through it all a second time?

Hell, I thought.

I put the drink down. I called the waiter over and paid the check.

I was out on the street before I realized I had won my greatest victory.

Because it was a victory. Miraculously, I had sloughed off all the deadening weight of anxiety. I was no longer Peter Duluth in his tight little sheath of despair, suffering as no man had ever suffered before. I was just a guy in a jam—a guy who had better do something about it quickly.

Wasn't there a breed of spider which paralyzed its victims with a poisoned bite and kept them alive but passive for the eventual meal? That was the Nanny-spider. But Nanny's numbing venom had not been quite powerful enough. I was tougher than she had thought.

I felt an improbable exhilaration which brought an extraordinary clarity of mind. I had not seduced Nanny Ordway. Iris and everyone thought that I had. I had almost come to believe it myself. But I had not seduced Nanny Ordway.

When her poison had been in my veins and I had been the willing victim, I had decided that she must have been mad because that was the only explanation which could still make me guilty—of folly and obtusity. But suddenly, like all the other bugaboos, that one too was exorcized. Why had I gone on trying so futilely to prove Nanny Ordway had been mad? Lieutenant Trant didn't think she had been mad. Miss Amberley, John Amberley, had both been sure of her sanity. And hadn't I too been sure of it when she'd been alive? For the first time in days I started to have confidence again in my own judgment of character. Nanny Ordway had been sly, perhaps, double-faced, scheming. But of course she had not been mad.

Lieutenant Trant thought she had been murdered. Okay. Why wasn't that a solution no more unlikely than a solution of suicide? And why wasn't it, instead of being another stone around my neck, a lifeline to pull me to safety? For, if she had been murdered, I hadn't murdered her. Someone else had. Someone who must have hung her to my chandelier and left her there to victimize me.

If that was the way it had happened, Nanny Ordway was not the only Enemy. There was another Enemy who was not a ghost, who was alive and who could still be grappled with.

Taxis were streaming up Broadway. I flagged one and had it drive me home.

The telephone was ringing when I entered the apartment. I went to answer it. Miss Mills' voice said:

"Peter, where on earth have you been? I've been calling for half an hour."

"Did you see Trant?"

"Yes, I saw him and . . ." She broke off.

"And—what?"

"It's bad, Peter. It couldn't be worse. I'm coming right over."

She hung up. If Miss Mills said it was bad, it was bad. Trant then had proved it was murder? He was going to arrest me? My new stability was not shaken. Peter Duluth, the phoenix risen from his own ashes! I lit a cigarette. I waited for her—quite calmly, confident there was something I could and would do.

She arrived in about ten minutes. She came running into the living-room. I'd never seen her distracted before. It touched me. Miss Mills and anxiety didn't go together.

I said, "Trant thinks it's murder and he thinks I murdered her?"

She gazed at me, startled. She had thought I'd be a nervous wreck, of course. All of them—all of the people who were fond of me—were still haunted by what had happened to me once.

I put my hands on her arms. "Is that it, Miss Mills?"

"Yes, Peter. I guess it is."

"He told you?"

"Oh, no. He's much too discreet for that."

She sat down on the arm of a chair and started fumbling ineffectually in her purse. I brought out cigarettes and lit one for her.

She said, "I went into his office in a fluttery, spinster

routine. I was worried, I said. So terribly worried with you unhappy and Lottie sick. Couldn't something be done? Right away I saw some papers on his desk. I thought they might be something. I pretended to work myself into a vapor. I asked for a glass of water. He went out into the squad-room to get it for me. I ran around the desk to look at the papers and . . ."

"And?"

"It was a report from a handwriting expert. About the drawings. Peter, the suicide note was a fake. The "secret of love"—all that—had just been torn off the title page of her story, the report said. And the drawing of the hanging girl—it hadn't been made by Nanny Ordway. The expert had checked it with the first drawing she'd done and he was sure. Someone else had made it. And —and at the end of the report, he'd written: 'So I guess you're right, Trant. It's murder.' "

She was looking at me miserably, still only half believing I could take it. "I was back in my chair before he came in with the water. And then, while I was drinking it, the phone rang. He was smooth as he could be, but I got enough. It was a Doctor Schwartz from the morgue, and I could tell Trant was excited. He kept on saying, yes, yes, good. And then, at the end, he said: 'So I'll call you at four-thirty for the final word.' It was obvious, Peter. It must have been something about the autopsy. Trant had put them on to something. They thought they'd proved it. But he'd have to wait for the final results."

She leaned forward on the chair arm. "Peter, darling, I left then. I rushed to the nearest telephone. I've been in the booth ever since. I hate to tell you this. But I've got to. It's you he's going to suspect. Of course it is. And once he's got the dope from the morgue. Once . . ."

He'll arrest you. That was what she had been meaning to say, but at that moment her words choked off in a sob. I put my arms around her, dimly astonished at the shift in mood which had me comforting the indomitable Miss Mills.

"Don't worry," I said. "I didn't kill her."

"Of course you didn't!" She looked up at me, her face passionately convinced. "Do you imagine there's anything in the world that could make me believe that? But . . ."

"It's all right. I promise you."

I glanced at my watch. It was a quarter of four. The chips were down now. Trant had proved the drawing was a fake. At four-thirty he would get the dope—whatever it was—from the morgue. After that, what was to prevent him from coming around to arrest me?

An hour or two hours, maybe. That was all. My shiny new calm was wonderful. I was in love with it. Francis Bacon was back again at my elbow, whispering: *"Knowledge is power."* There was one way, at least, to gain some knowledge—a way I couldn't try with Miss Mills there. I wasn't going to have Miss Mills implicated any more deeply than she was already.

I managed to get rid of her. She didn't want to go. She clung to me, begging me to let her stand by me, all the mother in her resenting the fact that I had suddenly grown up. I told her to go home and relax. She refused. Then, to make her feel useful, I suggested that she go back to the office, call Thomas Wood, and tell him I wouldn't be able to take him to the theater that evening.

"There's still the play, Miss Mills. You don't want me to go penniless to jail."

That, and a promise to call her whenever I needed her, did the trick.

It was four o'clock when she left. Immediately afterwards, I called the morgue and asked for Dr. Schwartz.

This was like a fiasco at dress-rehearsal, I thought. When things got bad enough, you coped with them because you had to. I felt absolutely sure of myself and of my own faked voice when I said:

"Schwartz? Trant here. Any news?"

"Oh, Trant, I was just going to call you. You're clear on the neck marks. Even Doctor Duntun agrees now. Once he heard you'd proved the suicide note was a fake, he came around to murder. It still could just have been suicide, but it's much more likely she was garroted first and then strung up. Don't worry about any defense tricks. We can make a case that'll hold up in any court of law in the country."

"Fine." I took a gamble. "And the other thing?"

Dr. Schwartz laughed. "You hit it right on the nose. Final report's just come down. So much for your friend's innocent line about never having touched her! She was pregnant all right. Between five and six weeks pregnant. That make you feel good? So far as we're concerned, it's all sewed up, Trant. Go grab your theatrical producer whenever you want to. And good hunting."

I put down the receiver. I was enough of a would-be actor still to feel for a few seconds that I actually was Lieutenant Trant. I was sitting in that little monk's cell of an office, smiling my thin smile of justice-triumphant. Here at last was the final piece of evidence. Peter Duluth, the seducer, who had killed his pregnant light-of-love before she could wreck his marriage!

Of course that was what Trant would think. It was what the world would think. But for me, back being Peter Duluth, again, this was the final defeat of Nanny Ordway. Gone forever was the innocent, pixie Gloria O'Dream. *A man and a girl can be friends*. All the tormenting bafflements of the case had dissolved and the true Nanny Ordway was starting to emerge from the mists.

She had been five or six weeks pregnant. She had suspected, then, what the situation might be almost from the beginning of our relationship. So much for her broken confession to Miss Amberley; so much for her terrible, quiet sleep in my bed; so much for her noble, soap-opera letter to Iris.

Sure, I had been her victim, but not just the victim of a mad girl with a mad infatuation. I had been a far more humiliating kind of victim than that.

She had decided she was pregnant and she had picked me for the father. Peter Duluth, the ideal sucker to be on the other end of a paternity suit efficiently supported by the evidence of her girl-friend, the evidence of my maid, even the evidence of my own wife!

Here at last was a plausible Nanny Ordway. Why had I never thought of her before? Had it been my vanity? Had I secretly preferred the picture of a moonstruck maiden dying for love of me to a portrait of myself as a middle-aged fool on the wrong side of a shakedown?

In the fatuous excitement of having at last discovered the truth, I thought: So it's all over. Trant doesn't have to come for me. I'll go to Trant. I'll explain it all to him. I can explain it all to Iris, to Lottie. Suddenly, out of the blue, I had written a last act where Peter Duluth lived happily ever after with a loving wife, an adoring star in a smash hit, an abject, apologizing police detective . . .

That was where the bubble burst. Just because I had realized at last that I'd been the victim of a plot, that did not automatically save me from being the victim. Of course I could go to Trant, to Iris, to all of them and yell: *I'm not the father of her child. Goody, goody.* But why should they believe me? It was ludicrous to suppose they would. Wasn't I ever going to learn that the truth isn't enough—that the truth needs as much evidence to support it as a lie?

Why wasn't I the father? How could I prove it—unless I found the father?

And how was I to pick the father out of all the men in New York?

Sylvia's. Sylvia's on West Tenth Street. It was the flimsiest of clues to Nanny Ordway's past, but it was the only one I had. It was better to try Sylvia's again then to sit here and wait for the cold, relentless servant of the Law.

I put on my coat. I was a fugitive from justice. At least, I would be one from the moment Trant called the morgue. But my exhilaration was still with me.

It was because Nanny Ordway had gone. The spectral, accusing hand was no longer in mine. The suggestion of her grave little-girl profile was no longer there at the corner of my eye. I was free of my obsession.

The Nanny-spider was dead.

CHAPTER SIXTEEN

It was five o'clock when I reached Sylvia's and it was still closed. There was no reason why a nightclub should be open that early in the evening, but the fact that it had been dark and locked the night before was ominous. A cop was chatting with a news vendor on the corner. Soon, I thought, all the cops in Manhattan would be after me. It amused me to ask a cop for help. I went up to him and said:

"When does Sylvia's open?"

"Sylvia's?" He glanced at me, amiably, without interest. "It shut down. Couple of weeks ago. Sylvia went off to California. Got a new place there."

I exploited my disappointment. "What am I going to do? I'm from out of town. Left a coat there about a month ago."

"If you left a coat, you'd better go around to the station-house. Lost and Found. Maybe they sent it over there."

"No. I don't think so. You see, I left it on purpose. With the hat-check girl." Hat-check girls know everything there is to know about the place they work in. "She was a pal of mine. I suppose you don't know . . ."

"Anne?" cut in the news vendor. "Good-looking girl? Colored?"

"That's it," I said.

"Well, that's a cinch. Anne's working just around the

corner, now. Short-order lunch counter. Halfway down the block. Can't miss it. You're in luck, mister."

"Yes," I said, sincerely returning his grin. "I'm in luck. Thank you. Thanks, officer."

I hurried around the block. The light was fading. Kids were playing ball against a blind wall. There was only one short-order lunch counter. *Joe's Quick Lunch.* I dodged a woman with a perambulator and went into it. Three girls in white uniforms waited behind a long tiled counter. Only one was colored. She was on the end of the counter near the door. As I entered, she glanced up from washing dirty glasses.

The news vendor had been right. She was astonishingly beautiful. It was a face suggesting jungle leaves, waterfalls in forest pools, exotic flowers drooping from vines, a face Gaugin would have painted if he had gone to Leopoldville instead of Tahiti. Her eyes, green behind thick black lashes, watched me with a weary passivity as if dirty glasses, Danish pastry, men and women were all things of equal and equally transitory unimportance.

"Yes, sir?" she asked.

I said, "Your name's Anne, isn't it? You worked at Sylvia's?"

"That's right."

"Did you know Nanny Ordway?"

There was no change in the dazed, dreamy eyes. "Are you a cop?"

"No."

Her gaze, studying my face, kindled to faint interest. "You're Peter Duluth. I saw your picture in the paper."

"You did know Nanny?"

"Sure, I knew her."

"Then will you help me—please?"

Her dark red lips parted, showing a glimpse of white teeth. It wasn't exactly a smile, but it removed the barrier of detachment. It was as if I wasn't a dirty glass or a piece of Danish pastry any more. "I guess you're in a jam, Mr. Duluth."

"That's right."

"I'll talk to you." She glanced toward the other girls. "But not here. The old man's death on talking with customers. I'm through at eight."

"No," I said. "It's got to be now."

I took out my wallet. She glanced across the counter at it indifferently. "Save your money," she said. And then: "Okay. Make like you're a cop and come with me."

She emerged from behind the counter and led me past the few spindly tables to a back room where an old Italian with a thick mat of white hair was moving crates of Coca-Cola around.

He glanced up at us sharply. "Yes?" he said. "Yes, yes, yes?"

"Pop," said Anne. "I got to go out a while. It's the cops. They want to talk to me."

I imitated Lieutenant Trant's brisk severity. The old man peered at me uneasily.

"Cops?"

"That's it," I said.

"Anne," he said. "She's a good girl. She ain't done nothing wrong."

"No," I said. "We just need her help."

"She's a good girl," he repeated. He turned to Anne, his old face glossed with anxious affection. "Don't you let 'em do anything bad, Anne."

"No, Pop."

"You want I should go with you—tell 'em what a good girl you are?"

"No, Pop. It's okay."

He shook his head mournfully. "Okay, then. Okay." He swung back to me. "But you treat her right, mister, and you bring her back quick."

"Sure," I said. "Get your coat, Anne."

I went out of the place and waited on the sidewalk. Soon Anne came out wearing over her uniform an old brown coat with a fur collar that would have made any other girl look drab.

"Let's go to my place," she said. "It's just across West a bit."

We crossed the darkening Seventh Avenue, turned into a little cul-de-sac, and stopped in front of an old brownstone house with a dirty glass door. Anne opened the door with a key. A dim light revealed a dingy hall and a naked, even dingier staircase. An old woman with a mutt on a tartan leash came out of a side room. She blinked at us disinterestedly as we went up the stairs. There was a sour smell of poverty.

On the second floor, Anne opened a door.

"Come on in."

She turned on a light to combat the twilight. The room was just about as small as a room could be. A bed took up almost all the space. A little dresser was jammed in a corner. There was a red paper shade over the ceiling bulb. A small radio stood on the window sill.

And I'd felt paternal and guilty at Nanny Ordway's having to rough it in the Amberley apartment!

Anne took off her coat and hung it on a peg behind the door.

"Sit down on the bed. It's okay."

I sat down. She crossed to the other side of the bed and sat by the radio. She wasn't embarrassed about the room or the poverty. I suppose she accepted it just the way she accepted everything else.

She picked up her purse and brought out a pack of cigarettes. I offered her mine, but she said:

"That's okay. Save them."

I took out my lighter. She leaned toward it, inhaling. The flame from the lighter made a little circle of brightness on her chin. It was a chin for a Pharaoh's daughter. I wondered how it felt to be as beautiful as that and to live in this room.

She was looking at me with a kind of impersonal compassion as if I was just another member of the great army of the distressed.

"Well, honey, just how bad's the trouble?"

"Bad. You read about it?"

"Sure."

"Nanny didn't kill herself. She was murdered."

There was no flicker in the quiet green eyes. "Sure she was murdered. That's the first thing I thought when I read it in the papers."

I felt a flurry of excitement. "Why?"

"Nanny kill herself? Not that one. Not in a million years. She was too busy."

"Busy?"

"Busy to get on, to get up, to get some place. First day she came to work at the club I got her number—making up to Sylvia, acting so folksy with the other girls, even with me. Anne, dear, this. Anne, darling, that. The sweetheart of Sigma Chi. Look at her with those Amberleys."

"What about the Amberleys?"

She shrugged. "Just to show how she operated. One evening she came in early. She always came in early. Sylvia liked that. And she stopped off at the checkroom. Most times she always did that too, to prove how democratic she was. And this day, she said, 'You know that Miss Amberley who's always come in, Anne, darling? I've just been reading the Social Register in a bookstore and she's in it. The Amberleys. A big, grand family in Boston.' And I said, 'So what?' And she said, 'Probably they're rich and there's an unmarried brother too.' She laughed, made like she was kidding. But right after that Miss Amberley and her brother were in. No sooner you could turn around, Nanny was waiting on them and it not even her table. Next day she'd moved in on them."

Fascinated, I said, "That's how it happened with the Amberleys?"

"Sure." Anne's golden fingers were moving up and down on the bedspread as if she were playing some imaginary tune. "Nanny didn't have to keep up a front with me. I was just the hat-check girl. All the time it was that way. 'Who's that one, Anne? Is there anything there, Anne?' Once Errol Flynn was in. You should have seen her. Almost bust a gut wiggling her hips. Offered me two bucks to let her give him his coat when he left. Celebrities. Anything with a bank account. Get on the gravy train. That was Nanny."

There she was at last. The real Nanny Ordway—the Nanny who had hidden so cunningly behind Miss Amberley's "best friend," John Amberley's "Henry James lover," my "Gloria O'Dream." The real Nanny. The Nanny-spider.

I said, "The Amberleys were crazy about her."

"So was Sylvia. So were all of them."

"John Amberley even asked her to marry him. She stalled him off."

"Why not? Keep him on ice. If no one bigger and better comes along, okay. If someone bigger and better does come along . . ."

"Me, for example?"

She looked up again gravely from her fingers on the bedspread. "That's the way it went, wasn't it?"

"Yes."

"What was she after with you anyway? To hook you?"

"I guess so."

"That's what I thought first thing. A big producer. A celebrity. If you'd ever come in the club, you'd have got an Errol Flynn routine. Who cares you were married to a glamorous movie star? That wouldn't have fazed Nanny. Nanny was a pushover for Nanny. Thought she was Garbo and Rita Hayworth rolled into one. Miss Irresistible." She paused. "And then what?"

It was all as clear now as if it had been recorded on film.

"I suppose she figured she couldn't hook me, after all. So she switched."

"To a shake-down?"

"That's it. She was pregnant."

The dreamy, unjoltable green eyes studied my face. "By you?"

"God, no. I never touched her. But I was the sucker she'd picked for the father. Paternity suit."

Anne nodded. For a moment she sat on the bed in silence, beautiful, magnificent—the Emperor's daughter who had put on the lunch-counter uniform as a whimsical disguise. Suddenly she said, "So that's why you killed her?"

There had been no censure in her voice, not the faintest trace of anything but the obvious need of stating an obvious fact. I thought of all the other accusations which had been hurled at me during the last days. Seducer, from Lottie. Coward, from Miss Amberley. Liar, from Iris. None of them had accused me of being a murderer. This should have been the final humiliation. But it wasn't. Not from Anne.

I said, "I didn't kill her."

She accepted my word just as simply as she had offered the accusation.

"But the cops think you did?"

"They're going to arrest me any minute. They have all the evidence in the world. That's why I wanted to talk to you."

"Why?"

"She had a key. She could have taken anyone to my apartment. That's what she must have done. She must have taken someone there. And it must have been the father of the child. That's who killed her. The father. And I thought . . ."

"I might know someone?"

"Yes."

She shook her head. "That was six months ago she was working at the club, honey."

"I know, but . . ."

"And me the hat-check girl? I wasn't grand enough to meet her friends."

I had forgotten some of the urgency. The tour into Nanny's past had blurred it. But now it came rushing back. Was my luck with the news vendor, my luck at the lunch counter going to lead, after all, to a blind alley?

"You don't know any man in her life?"

"Mr. Amberley."

"No one else?" Clutching at straws, I remembered part of the Amberley's touching saga of Nanny's life. *She was rooming with another girl. It was all very inconvenient for her.* "What about the girl she was living with before she moved in with the Amberleys?"

"Girl!" Anne echoed. "That wasn't a girl. It was a man."

"You're sure?"

"Yes. She made like it was a girl. At the club she was always talking about her roommate. But one payday she was sick. She called down, asked me to pick up her pay envelope for her. She needed it, she said. She told me the address. I took the pay up. There was a man's name on the buzzer and a man came to the door and took the money. Later Nanny said not to tell the others. It was her uncle, she said. But it didn't look good, living with a man in such a small place. That's what she said."

Was this a lead, or just another instance of Nanny's duplicity? I asked, "And the man? Who was he?"

"Gee, I don't remember the name. It was like a year ago maybe. But he was kind of older. Good-looking, but older with whole lots of hair."

"And the apartment?"

"On East 38th Street. Number 38, was it? Yes, that's it. I remember. 38 East 38th Street. Second floor."

That wasn't much, but it was something. "That's all?"

"Yes, I guess that's all."

I got up from the bed.

"You're going to try it?"

"Sure."

She got up too. She came around the bed and stood close to me.

"Well, good luck."

She smiled. It was the first time she had smiled. And I thought: Of all the people I know, here's the only one who's trusted me.

"Thanks, Anne. Thanks a lot."

I glanced around the dreary little room, at the red paper shade on the bulb, at the radio on the chipped window sill.

I said, "I wish there was something . . ."

"There!" Her voice broke in, soft, soothing, a mother's voice. "You got enough trouble, honey. Don't you start to worry about me. I got my room. I got my job. Isn't anyone can push me around. I'm okay. Goodbye, Mr. Duluth."

"Goodnight, Anne."

CHAPTER SEVENTEEN

A taxi dropped me at 38th Street and Madison. I had bought a paper. I had half expected a headline: ORDWAY CASE CRACKED. PETER DULUTH SOUGHT. But there was nothing in the news about Nanny at all. That was Trant, of course. The theatrical flourish was not for him. He would always get his man before he broke his story.

It was about seven o'clock. My self-assurance was still intact, although I did not have much hope from an address casually remembered by a girl who had only visited it once. A man Nanny had been living with a year ago! An older man! An "uncle"! That didn't sound like the lover for whom I was searching. It sounded more like just another victim—an earlier host on whom the parasite had battened before she had discovered the Amberleys. The street was deserted. A large vacant lot on the corner helped to bring an atmosphere of desolation. I found the house and walked up steps into the little entrance hall.

Second floor, Anne had said. It was dark, and the names under the buzzers were old and blurred. I lit my lighter and moved the flame along the printed cards. First floor front . . . First floor rear . . . Second floor rear . . .

I looked at the name under the buzzer and excitement shot through me.

The name on the card was:

Gordon Ling.

Although Gordon had been working in *Star Rising*, I hadn't had the faintest idea of where he lived. Now I thought of Anne's description—older, good-looking with lots of hair. It fitted exactly. And Gordon, right there in my play, was no shadowy figure from Nanny's past. He was as immediate as I.

I remembered almost the first words Nanny had ever spoken to me. *I came with some people. They've gone off being glamorous.* Gordon had been at that party. Of course! Gordon had brought her to Lottie's. The flashy, near-failure actor, the little girl on the make—an ideally suited couple—going together to the grand party. Why? For Nanny to pick up a suitable victim for a planned paternity suit?

Gordon Ling.

My luck was sticking with me, after all.

I pressed the buzzer. An answering click sounded in the front door. I pushed the door inward and almost ran up the stairs.

Before I could knock at the apartment, Gordon Ling opened the door. He was wearing a bright silk robe over his pants and shirt. When he saw me, his professional smile of welcome faded giving way to a look of acute uneasiness.

"Peter!"

"Yes," I said. "Me."

I pushed past him into the little living-room. It was all aggressively masculine with leather and pewter and pipe racks, as if he was hoping to be photographed in front of it and called "distinguished" by *Harper's Bazaar*. The walls were plastered with theatrical photographs. Bankhead . . . Hayes . . . A picture of Iris caught my eye. *To Gordon. Good Luck. Iris Duluth.* Had Iris worked in a play with Gordon? I couldn't remember.

The sight of her calm, familiar face, interjected at that moment, was disturbing.

Gordon came hurrying after me. "Peter, what is it you want?"

"What do you think I want? I've come about Nanny Ordway."

He scurried around a chair until he was in front of me. He was fluttery almost like an old woman. It didn't go with the handsome chiseled features and the pipe racks.

"But you shouldn't be here. The police—they've only just left."

"The police?"

"Lieutenant Trant. He was here—ten minutes ago."

"Why?" I asked.

He ran a hand through his thick black hair. It was a typical, hammy gesture. I'd tried to cure him of it a hundred times at rehearsals. "About Nanny, of course. He'd found out, too. The way you have, I guess. From Sylvia in California."

"Found out what?"

"About Nanny and me. That Nanny was my niece."

His niece! Then Nanny hadn't lied to Anne after all. So much for my "brilliant" theory. Depression took hold of me.

"You were her uncle?"

"Isn't that what you came about?"

I sat down on one of the red leather chairs. "No. But it'll have to do. Tell me."

"But, Peter . . ."

"Tell me."

He moistened his lips. "You mean—what? What I know about Nanny?"

"Of course."

"Peter, you mustn't be mad at me. I tried to do the

right thing." He was twisting the tasseled ends of his bathrobe cord—like Lottie twisting her pearls. Actors, I thought. They're all the same. Without direction, they stink. "Honest, Peter, I didn't mean . . ."

"Just tell me, Gordon."

He picked up a highball glass which still had some liquor in it. I guess he felt easier with a prop.

"Well, it isn't much, really. I mean—I'd always known she was around. I mean, she was my sister's child and when my sister and her husband died a couple of years ago—well, there was Nanny. But she was in Virginia and she was living with some friends of the family and . . . maybe I should have helped out a bit. But I wasn't doing so good at the time and I figured she'd be okay. And she was, I guess. Until about a year ago, when the people got broke or something. That's when she came here. She didn't even write. Just one morning, here she was. She'd come to New York, she said, to get a job."

The glass was helping him. It made him feel like a man of distinction again. He started pacing up and down the room. This was not what I'd come for. But, in spite of the urgency which grew more extreme every minute, it had its own fascination. Here, at last, I was learning about Nanny Ordway's initial step onto the scene—her first entrance, the little girl from Virginia, slipping into Gordon Ling's apartment with her suitcase. "Uncle, I've come to get a job. . . ."

"Of course I took her in, Peter. My only niece. Anyone'd do that. This place isn't big at all and I hadn't planned . . . but she seemed like a nice enough kid, quiet, helpful, didn't want to be a drain on me financially. Getting her a job wasn't easy. She didn't know anything, wasn't trained to anything. Wanted to be a writer, matter of fact. But I fixed it at last—with Sylvia. Sylvia and I had been buddies a long time. Played a whole winter with her once in a club in L.A. Sylvia took her in for my sake. And Nanny was fine about it— the job, I mean, bringing back her pay every week, helping out. But—well, a guy likes his own life, you know what I mean? Having a niece right there, it's okay, but . . . She knew that. She was fine about that, too. After a couple of months, she met up with some friend . . . that Amberley girl, and moved in with her."

Yes, all that was right. The quiet first act. The slow build-up. The mousy, good little niece. "Here's my pay envelope, Uncle. Can I do the dishes tonight, Uncle? Uncle, I don't want to be a burden on you. I'm moving in with a girl-friend." The Nanny-spider had still been in disguise. So far there were only glimpses of menace. "Anne, darling, here's two bucks. Let me give Errol Flynn his coat. Anne, dearest, that Miss Amberley, she's in the Social Register. A grand family from Boston."

I watched Gordon. I thought: He isn't lying. He's not a good enough actor to deceive me. This is the way it happened between Nanny and him; and this is how he had thought of her—and probably still does. The good, quiet niece. Gordon had been another victim.

"That's all?" I asked.

"Yes, that's all of the beginning."

I said, "Why didn't you go to the police when you heard she was dead?"

He flushed—it was a bright, unnatural flush like rouge. "I had my reasons. I was only doing . . . Peter, it seemed the only way under the circumstances. And— and I didn't know then that she'd been murdered."

"But you know now?"

"Yes. Lieutenant Trant told me this evening."

"And you know she was pregnant?"

"Yes, I knew that."

I said, "It was her lover who killed her."

"That's what Trant thinks."

"Do you know who her lover was?"

I had said that just to say it. I hadn't had the slightest hope that it would get me anywhere. But Gordon stopped in his tracks. He stood in front of me, looking down at hands that seemed suddenly clumsier than ever.

"Yes, Peter, I know."

I said, "Tell me."

"Peter, do I have to?"

"Tell me."

"But . . ."

"To hell with any buts."

He looked up. His face was still flushed and miserable. "Honest, Peter, I wasn't prying. When she left to live with Miss Amberley, I knew she still had a key to this place. That was okay with me. She even left some of her stuff here. After you'd given me the job in *Star Rising,* she came around backstage a couple of times to see me, but that was all. I was leading my life. I was letting her lead hers."

"Did you take her to that party at Lottie's?"

"What party? Oh, no. I just saw her there. Across the room. Didn't even get a chance to speak to her. And it was after that, anyway, that I started noticing . . . I mean, about the matinee afternoons . . ."

He broke off.

"Matinee afternoons?"

"You know, I'd come back after the show tired. Wouldn't notice much. Sometimes, maybe, I thought the place looked kind of different—too neat sometimes, not neat enough other times. But for quite a while I didn't stumble to it at all. Then it started to dawn on me. Somebody's been here, I thought. Someone's coming here every matinee afternoon and then sometimes in the evenings too. I thought right away of Nanny, of course. Who else could it be? I wasn't going to make a fuss or anything. Hell, if Nanny needed a place away from the Amberley girl to be alone—it didn't interfere with me. But I wanted to be sure.

"She'd told me not to call her at Miss Amberley's. I guess she hadn't told her she had an uncle in New York. Maybe she figured she'd be thrown out if Miss Amberley knew she had some place else to go. So I wrote her a note and asked her to come around. When she came, I asked point blank: Have you been coming here? She was just as frank with me. She had a boy-friend, she said—and there were reasons why she couldn't entertain him at Miss Amberley's. She should have asked me, she said. But she hadn't thought I would mind . . . and, Peter, I didn't go into it, honest. God knows, I'm not the heavy uncle. If the kid had a lover—more power to her. I told her it was okay . . . to go right ahead. And that was that."

Once again my hopes were rising. Gordon wasn't the man but he was leading directly toward him. This then had been the center of the Nanny-spider's web. Here, secret from the Amberleys, secret from everyone, she had brought her lover and planned with him the scheme which eventually had taken form as the destruction of Peter Duluth.

Gordon Ling was looking at me earnestly, with an embarrassment I found both baffling and unsettling.

"I'd never have known, Peter, if it hadn't been for that last time. Just—just the day before she died when she came here and . . ."

Once again he gave up. Infected by his uneasiness, I asked:

"Came here—and what?"

"Well," he blurted, "she told me everything. Poor

kid, probably she was as much to blame as anyone, but you couldn't help being sorry for her. She was in such a state, carrying on, half out of her mind, sobbing her heart out. She told me it all, how desperately in love she was, how she'd hoped for the divorce, how she'd realized it couldn't ever be and the only thing was for her to give it up, how she'd tried to be brave but how it was hopeless now because she was almost sure she was going to have a baby. Could I help her? She begged it over and over again. Couldn't I please do something?"

That was the sort of dramatic scene which normally Gordon thought he did well. But he was terrible at it now as if he'd played it out of town to disastrous notices and had lost his nerve.

"After all, Peter, I was her uncle. It was up to me to do something. I tried to calm her down. I tried to comfort her. I said, 'You've got to tell me this guy's name. If he's responsible for all this, if you really love him, if you're really going to have a baby, he's got to get a divorce and marry you. Don't worry,' I said. 'I'll go to him. I'll make him see he's got to do it. Tell me his name.' "

Hope had made me slow-witted. I realized that then. With shocking clarity, the reason behind his excruciating embarrassment dawned on me.

"So she told you his name, Gordon?"

He was looking down sheepishly at the carpet. "That's right."

He came suddenly to me and gripped my hands. We were the two sophisticated men-about-town helping each other through a difficult scene.

"Honest, Peter, I'd never dreamed it was you. When she told me . . . God, you can imagine how I felt. I'd said I'd stand by her. I was her uncle. There she was crying, talking about suicide. I knew it was my duty.

But—with Iris and you . . . I mean, when you'd been so good to me, giving me my first big part in years and . . ."

"Yes," I said, "yes, yes, I know."

And, of course, I knew. Why hadn't I realized it from the beginning of his monologue? The Nanny-spider had woven an Amberley web to catch me, a Lucia web, an Iris web. Of course she would have woven a Gordon web too. Almost laughably Gordon had been designed as the last and most convincing witness in the paternity suit—the indignant uncle storming in loco parentis. "You've seduced my niece. She's pregnant. I demand recompense."

"So you see." Laughably, too, Gordon was trying to propitiate me. "I didn't pry, Peter. It was all thrown at me. It—it was terribly awkward. I stalled, of course. I— well, I really didn't do much of anything that night. And then the next evening, Lottie came to the theater and—and I heard."

His vivid blue eyes, which were only a little faded, fixed my face with an "honest" desire for criticism, for castigation.

"Maybe you think I did wrong, Peter. I don't know. Hell, I don't know anything any more. I'm so mixed up. But I heard she was dead, that she was hanging there from your chandelier. It was dreadful, of course. But— well, it was done, wasn't it? You see, I thought she'd committed suicide. We all did. And I thought: Poor kid—then she really did it. She's killed herself for Peter. And I thought too: Well, Peter's in bad enough already. If I go to the police, I'd have to tell the whole story. What good would it do? I mean—it wouldn't help Nanny. And with Peter always so considerate of me . . ."

The honest eyes were still unwinkingly on my face.

The voice broke off with a noble tremble. Poor Gordon, the actor to the end! He'd thought his niece had killed herself because a producer had seduced her, but he'd still been realistic enough to remember that a producer was a producer.

I said, "So you decided not to go to the police at all— for my sake?"

"Yes, Peter." A quick smile came. "Yes, boy. That's it."

"But now—this evening—you've told all this to Trant?"

The smile fled and the sincere expression was back.

"Peter, I hated to. Honest, I did. But when he said it was murder! That's serious. You can get into terrible trouble if you hold back evidence on murder."

"Sure," I said. "Sure you can, Gordon."

I looked at him. I thought gloomily of Lieutenant Trant. He had everything now—a handwriting expert to say the suicide note was a fake, the M.E. to say the hanging had been phony—and now Gordon Ling, the "victim's" uncle with a story as good as a death warrant for me.

Lieutenant Trant, the seeker after Truth, had at last drawn up the naked lady from the bottom of the well. That's what he thought. He hadn't really, of course. All he'd drawn up had been a dummy strategically planted there by Nanny Ordway—and her killer.

But that made no difference so far as I was concerned. To all intents and purposes, I was trapped.

I said, "Okay, Gordon, I've only one thing to say. Two things. I never had anything to do with Nanny Ordway. And I didn't kill her."

He jumped at that. I didn't for a moment think he believed me, but it was the perfect cue to shake off "uncle" and become the producer's little pal again.

"Of course, Peter, I never thought you did. That's

what I told Trant right away. 'Peter a murderer?' I said. 'Why, that's crazy.'"

For a moment, some of the Nanny-spider's poison seemed to be back in my veins. Give up. What's the use? But anger came to my rescue. Hell, I thought. I'm not going to let Nanny Ordway and Lieutenant Trant defeat me. There must be some way.

But the way wasn't here—in this sham little apartment with this sham sycophantic actor.

I got up.

Sharply Gordon said, "Peter, you're going?"

He hadn't meant to read relief into that line, but it was there.

"That's right," I said.

"But—but where?" He clutched my arm—the Scarlet Pimpernel's best friend warning him against the tumbrel. "Peter, don't go to your apartment. Trant, he—I mean, he almost said he was going there to arrest you."

"No," I said. "I won't go to the apartment."

"Then—where?"

Where indeed? "Oh, somewhere," I said.

I went to the door. I passed the photograph of Iris. *To Gordon. Good luck. Iris Duluth.* Gordon came hurrying after me. It was the swishing skirt of the bathrobe, I decided, that made him seem so old-womanish.

"Peter, I won't tell them you were here. Honest I won't."

"Thanks, Gordon."

"And you're not mad at me? You do see . . . ? Under the circumstances . . . ?"

"Yes, Gordon. I see."

CHAPTER EIGHTEEN

I was out again on 38th Street. My session with Gordon had not been entirely barren. At least I knew for certain now that Trant, like me, believed that Nanny had been killed by her lover. The only difference was that Trant was convinced that the lover had been I.

I started to walk down Madison Avenue. I came to a drugstore and went into it. Even a fugitive from justice has to eat. I sat at the fountain and ordered coffee and a sandwich. A couple of teen-aged girls were chattering over parfaits. *"Really, he's a screwball. A real screwball."* A woman with a poodle was getting stamps out of a stamp machine. No one paid me any attention. Why should they—yet? I looked just like anyone else.

Proof, I thought. Trant had all the proof. I had none. I knew that Nanny had taken her lover to her uncle's apartment. But how could I prove that I hadn't been the lover? Gordon, for all his protests of sympathy, couldn't help. He had stumbled on the fact that someone had been using his place only after the party at Lottie's—after I had actually met Nanny Ordway. If only he had noticed it earlier, that would have proved something. But he hadn't.

It all boiled down to a question of time.

The teen-aged girls went out together arm-in-arm. *"Crazy? Is that character crazy?"*

When she died, Nanny had been five or six weeks pregnant. How long had I actually known her? That was easy. I had met her the day Iris left for Jamaica. October 6th. And she had been killed on November 9th. How long was that? Four weeks and six days. The tiniest margin of one day! That wasn't enough to prove anything to anyone. If only there was another date—a date that could definitely place Nanny with a lover before the sixth of October.

Suddenly, as I sipped my coffee, I thought of John Amberley. He'd told me he had proposed to Nanny on his birthday. And Claire Amberley—hadn't she said just after his announcement. *"That was when I made her confide in me, the day she had told John to wait. I knew there was another man. I'd suspected it for some time."*

For some time *before* her brother's birthday! If John Amberley's birthday had been before October 6th, that would be proof.

I got up and paid my check at the cashier's desk, tangling with the leash of the poodle whose mistress was now hovering around the rack of Pocket Books. Hope was in the saddle again. Maybe Miss Amberley, my most merciless enemy, would turn out to be my savior after all. I picked up a taxi on Madison. I said:

"31 Charlton Street."

I knew Miss Amberley too well now to take any chances with her. Down in the submerged little foyer of Number 31, I pressed the buzzer for the apartment above hers. The click came in the door. I hurried up the stairs to her apartment and knocked. I was so sure now that my luck was holding that it never occurred to me she might be out. I felt no surprise or relief when her voice came from inside.

"Who is it?"

"Trant," I said in the voice that had done me service already that day. "Lieutenant Trant."

The door started to open. Before it was pulled more

than a quarter of the way inside, I pushed through and shut it behind me.

Miss Amberley was standing straight in front of me. She was wearing the same old paint-stained smock. Does she live in the thing? I thought. Her bulging green eyes, hard as metal, were glaring at me with an expression of mingled indignation and alarm.

"You told me to drop in whenever I was in the neighborhood."

"I—I thought it was Lieutenant Trant."

"I said it was Lieutenant Trant." I took a step toward her. "I want you to help me."

"Help you!" she laughed. "If there was a desert, if there was a flask of water . . ."

"You'd let me die of thirst?"

"Yes," she said.

I looked at her. I wondered how it felt to have all that hatred. What Miss Amberley needs, I thought, was a good sharp shock.

I said, "You know, of course, that Nanny was murdered?"

"Murdered!" She echoed the word in a strange little piping gasp. Instinctively she cringed away from me. I took advantage of it.

"She was murdered and Trant's going to arrest me. He's looking for me now. I might just as well have two murders to my credit as one."

I had said that with obvious sarcasm, but, incredibly, she took it seriously as a threat. Her face seemed to dissolve into a pointless pattern of terror.

With a lightning movement that almost took me unawares, she spun around toward the telephone. I jumped on her and caught her wrists. Her arms quivered at my touch as if I were a leper.

"No . . . no . . . no."

"Will you help me?"

"Don't hurt me. Please. Don't hurt me."

"Will you tell me what I want to know?"

"Anything."

"Your brother proposed to Nanny on his birthday, didn't he?"

"Yes, yes. You know that. He told you."

"But, before that, you'd suspected she had a lover. Isn't that what you said? Before the birthday?"

"Yes, of course. Weeks before. I knew. Anyone can tell."

"When is your brother's birthday?"

She was struggling to free her wrists now, aimlessly, feebly, the way a chicken goes on fluttering after its head has been cut off.

"When," I repeated, "is your brother's birthday?"

"October," she said. "October the second."

October 2nd! And I had met Nanny Ordway on October 6th. It worked. I had pulled it off.

I said, "And right after that, on the same day, on October the second, you made her admit she had a lover?"

"Yes, that's right. I told you."

"But she didn't mention my name—not until much later?"

"No. I told you that too." For a moment her hatred of me got the better of her panic. "But it was you. Of course it was you. She didn't mention your name. But what difference does that make—when she described you."

"Described me?"

"Yes," said Miss Amberley. "The husband of a famous actress."

Even now, that moment of all the many startling moments of the day is most vivid in my mind. Because there, suddenly out of the blue, was a solution. It hit me with a staggering impact. I released Miss Amberley's wrists. She gave a gasp and ran backward away from me, stumbling down onto one of the cluttered studio couches.

I stood for a moment, trying to get my excitement under control. Suddenly Miss Amberley leaped from the couch to the phone.

"Quick," she screamed into the receiver. "Get me the police. Quick."

I hurried out of the apartment. As I ran down the stairs, I could still hear that voice, hoarse, triumphant now.

"The police . . . Get me the police. . . ."

There were a dozen different things to be thought of, but from them all, it was the image of Iris which rose up, dwarfing everything else. In the last few hectic hours, there had been no time to pamper my misery at the loss of my wife. But now that release had miraculously come, I could think only of Iris. She'd been to Alec's party. Certainly Alec had approached her about the play in England. Maybe, in her manufactured mood of hatred for me, she'd already signed to go to London. The thought sent a chill through me. I ran into a candy store and dialed her hotel. They told me she wasn't there. Then she was still at Alec's. Alec was at the Pierre. I found the number. I was put through to Alec's suite. His quiet, amiable voice said:

"Hello."

"Alec," I said. "This is Peter. Is Iris there?"

He paused a moment. "I'm sorry, Peter. She's just left."

The pause had given him away. "She's there," I said.

"No, she isn't."

"Alec, I've got to talk to her. It's desperately important. I . . ."

"One moment."

There was another pause. Then Iris' voice came, cool, studiedly hostile. "Really, Peter. Alec's in the middle of reading me his play."

"I've got to see you."

"But there's nothing to see me about. Couldn't you tell that at lunch?"

Didn't she know? Didn't everyone know by now?

I said, "Nanny was murdered."

I could hear her draw in her breath rapidly. "No."

"Trant's got all the evidence in the world. He's going to arrest me."

"Peter!"

"I've got to see you."

"Of course." It was wonderful to hear the old, natural voice, the unthinking sympathy. "Of course, Peter. I'll come right away. Where are you? At the apartment?"

"No. And we can't go there. Probably the police are watching it."

"Then where?" She paused. "How about Mother's? I have a key."

"That's fine."

"Then—then I'll just explain to Alec and come. Is it all right—I mean, to tell Alec?"

"Why not?"

"Then I'll be there."

She hung up. I went out again onto the street. Absurdly, I had half expected that the whole picture of the Village would have been changed by Miss Amberley's voice screaming: *Quick, the police.* . . . But nothing was altered. There was no commotion. I hurried to Sixth Avenue. I got in a taxi and told the driver to drive like hell to Iris' mother's apartment on 84th Street.

I knew Iris would be there ahead of me. She hadn't had so far to go. I took the elevator up to the 12th floor.

I knocked on the door. Iris opened it immediately. She was wearing a very grand cocktail dress. She had fixed herself up for Alec's party.

"Peter!"

She shut the door and led me into the living-room, which was fussily and eerily shrouded in dust covers against her mother's return from Jamaica.

She'd had time to think. She was a little suspicious. "Peter, you didn't make that up? If you did . . ."

"I didn't make it up."

I sat down on the back of one of the ghostly couches.

"She was murdered?"

"That's right."

"And Trant thinks you murdered her?"

"He knows it."

"The fool!"

The spontaneity with which she had said that banished my last, lingering anxieties.

"You don't think I killed her?" I said.

"You? Commit a murder? Don't be silly." She crossed and stood in front of me. There was a trace of a smile on her face. "Besides, you'd never be that dumb. Kill someone in your own apartment? Hang her from your own chandelier?"

There it was, the great reconciliation scene achieved with only a couple of lines of dialogue. I told her all I'd done since Miss Mills had brought me the news. I finished with Miss Amberley.

"You see? On October 2nd, Nanny admitted that she had a lover. I didn't meet her until October 6th, the day you left. That proves it, unless you think I was having a secret affair with her before you went away."

"Without my realizing it? There isn't a woman in the world who doesn't know when her husband's having an affair under her nose."

"There isn't?"

"Of course there isn't."

I had never thought it would be hard to convince Iris. Now the simple part was over. The difficult part was beginning. I got up off the couch.

I said, "Iris, baby. I know who it is. Nanny's lover. The man who killed her."

Her lips parted in astonishment.

"It's a cinch," I said. "There's no proof, but it's a cinch. Nanny used to go around backstage to see Gordon after *Star Rising* opened. He told me that. We know what she was like now, always on the prowl, trying to climb, fixated on celebrities. Gordon didn't take her to that party at Lottie's. How did she get there except through someone from the company? When Nanny admitted to Miss Amberley that she had a lover, four days before she'd met me, she gave the clue. She said her lover was the husband of a famous actress."

Iris was looking at me, half incredulous, half horrified. "You can't mean . . . Peter, not Brian!"

"Brian. Of course."

"No, Peter. It couldn't be Brian."

"Who else could it be?"

"But he's so sweet. He—he was always trying to help us."

"A conscience, maybe?"

Iris put her hand on my sleeve. "What are you going to do? Tell Trant?"

"With so little proof? A few stray sentences that nobody else heard? Do you expect Trant would believe me when he's got me pigeon-holed as the biggest liar, coward and libertine since Heliogabalus? And if it came to trial —think of the headlines, the photographers, especially with you in the middle of such a juicy scandal. No, it's better to go to Brian, to try and break him."

"You think you can?"

"I've got to. You call Lottie. Get her out of the apartment. Say you need her. Say you're unhappy. She'll come running."

"Now?"

"Yes, now."

She went to the phone. She talked for a few moments and hung up.

"It worked. Poor Lottie, she was thrilled. *I knew you'd need me.* She said it over and over again. And Brian's there. She's going to the hotel right away. I'll have to leave."

"So will I."

"But maybe Trant will be at the apartment, waiting for you."

"That's a chance I'll have to take."

She came to me suddenly, putting her arms around me. "Darling, how are you ever going to forgive me?"

"For what?"

"For the things I've said, for the things I've thought. For being a stinker. Peter. I didn't want to be. I wanted so hard not to be a stinker. And—in the end—I was worse than Lottie. Much worse. I'm sorry. Darling, I'm so sorry. . . ."

I kissed her on the shoulder, on the throat, and on the mouth. I thought: There's something to be said for unhappiness. It's so pleasant when it stops.

"Hurry, baby," I said. "You don't want Lottie to get there ahead of you."

CHAPTER NINETEEN

I went back to our apartment house. I had expected the police to be watching it. But there was no sign of them. Bill, rather sheepish, I thought, was on the elevator.

I said, "Take me up to Miss Marin's, will you, Bill?"

Everyone in the building talked about Miss Marin's apartment. Probably half of the employees didn't even know Brian's last name was Mullen. It was odd to feel depressed now that I was struggling out of the trap. But the switch had been too quick for me. From the beginning, Nanny had been the Enemy—Nanny, the scheming, sly little destroyer. I hadn't stopped feeling that way about her. And I hadn't yet stopped thinking of Brian as my friend.

It was a preposterously anachronistic attitude, of course. He wasn't my friend any more. He was a murderer who had pinned the blame for his crime on me. That was how I had to think of him. I had committed myself now.

He opened the door for me with his usual, cheerful grin. His hair was flopping down across his forehead. He was in shirtsleeves with a large white apron over his shirt and pants.

"Hi, Peter. Just been cleaning the bathroom. Lottie can create more chaos in five minutes. She's out, by the way. Iris called her. She forgot her nervous breakdown and ran."

"I know," I said. "I asked Iris to call her. I wanted to talk to you alone."

"Fine." His grin broadened. "Good news, I hope. I did my best with Iris this morning. Didn't think I got anywhere, but at least I tried." He put his big arm around my shoulders and drew me into the living-room. "What'll it be? Scotch? Rye? Scotch, of course."

He strolled over to Lottie's horrible chromium bar and poured drinks for both of us.

"Here, Peter." He sat down opposite me on a stool, crossing his knees. Brian was one of those men who can look boyish without looking silly. "Okay. What's on your mind?"

This wasn't at all the way the scene should have started. I looked at him, part of my confidence undermined by the atmosphere of friendly domesticity he had created. Could he really be as bland as this and still be guilty? Of course he could. It is only folklore to suppose that murderers are hounded by their consciences. They're insensitive. That's one of the reasons why they are murderers.

It was that insensitivity, that sublime self-assurance that I would have to work on. My hunch was not to mention murder. There was a good chance he didn't know that Trant had broken the suicide theory. I should be as bland as he. Blander.

I said, "I've just been talking to Gordon."

"Gordon? Gordon Ling?"

"He knows about you and Nanny, Brian." That was obviously the most effective lie. "He's found out you were the one she'd been taking to his place."

I had, I supposed, expected him to deny it or at least to be flustered. I was astonished when he merely threw out his hands with a wry little smile and said:

"So he tumbled to it, did he? I thought he would—

189

sooner or later." He paused. "He hasn't told Lottie, has he?"

"No."

"Thank God for that!" And then, "I'm glad you've found out. I should have told you long ago."

"You should?"

"Of course. But it was Lottie, Peter. I was scared to death she'd get on to it. And, with the suicide established and everything, I figured: Peter's in it anyway. How's it going to help him if I mess myself up in it too? Better for everyone if I keep my mouth shut. That's what I decided. You do understand? You don't think I'm too much of a heel?"

His expression had just the correct amount of rueful-ness and charm. He was even smoother than I had thought. I understood it all, of course. I had been right about his self-assurance and his underestimation of Trant. He thought that I and everyone else still believed in the suicide theory—so what was there to worry about? Gordon and I had found out he'd been mixed up with Nanny. But that was just another wrinkle to the suicide. He was calmly assuming that Gordon and I, as his friends, would never expose him just for the sake of exposing him, when the case was already closed.

I was going to get a neat little man-to-man admission. "Poor kid, maybe I was partly to blame."

And that would be that.

I said, "You'd better tell me about it."

"All of it, Peter? From the beginning?"

"Yes."

"Honest, if I'd thought I could have helped you by telling earlier . . ."

"Sure."

"Then you're not mad at me."

He smiled gratefully and, leaning forward, patted my knee.

And Lottie, I thought, had never let him be an actor!

"Now, when did I meet her?" He was puckering his forehead. "Can't exactly remember, but it was quite early in the run of *Star Rising*. It was one night just after curtain time. I'd been down at the theater with Lottie and was going home. I was coming out of the stage-door —and so was this girl. We walked together down the alley. I hardly noticed her, matter of fact. Then, suddenly, I felt her hand on my sleeve. 'Excuse me,' she said, 'but aren't you Charlotte Marin's husband?' I said: 'Sure.' She said: 'I thought so. Being Charlotte Marin's husband! How wonderful that must be!' We started talking then as we walked along. She told me she was Gordon's niece. I didn't have anything to do that evening. Almost before I realized it, I was asking her if she felt like dinner. She said: 'Oh, that would be marvelous. I could eat a bear.'"

In spite of the circumstances, I felt stealing over me the fascination which any new glimpse into Nanny Ordway's life always brought me. The parallel between Brian's first meeting with her and my own was terrifyingly close. The light hand on the sleeve—the oblique praise. . . . And then: *Oh, no, I don't want a drink, but I'm simply starved.* . . .

Brian's voice was running on. They had gone to a movie. They had inevitably made a second casual date— and then a third.

He looked up at me from the drink—earnestly. "You know, Peter? I guess you'll think this is a disloyal thing to say, but being married to Lottie—It's fine, of course. Couldn't be happier. But—well, when she's acting, it gets kind of lonely sometimes. We've got a whole raft of friends, of course. But they're all mostly Lottie's friends. Half the time I think they just put up with me because I'm Lottie's husband. So, it was pleasant to have found a kid like that, someone to pal around with when Lottie was at the theater."

They had met more and more often. Even though Brian had been careful to keep it all from Lottie, it had been a perfectly innocent relationship. And then, one afternoon, Nanny had invited him to tea at Gordon's.

For the first time a faint flush spread over his face. "That was when—when the other thing began, Peter. Even now, I don't quite know how it happened. But it did. And then, once it had happened—you can't imagine what it was like. I mean—the change in her. She was like a wild thing. She loved me, she said. She'd been crazy about me from the first moment she saw me. She'd love me forever. She'd die for me."

He got up from the stool. "I was in a hell of a stew. You don't have to believe this, but it's true. I'd never been unfaithful to Lottie before. I hadn't wanted to be. I was all mixed up and—and scared to death about Lottie. Because, if she found out . . . You know Lottie, Peter. You know the way she is."

I knew Lottie. I was beginning to know Brian. But, above all, I now knew Nanny Ordway supremely well. The Nanny-spider hadn't had only one technique for catching flies. There had been the "sincere" technique for the shy John Amberley; the pixie technique for the happily married Peter Duluth; the sexually flattering technique for Lottie's emasculated pet husband.

"I'd wanted to stop it right there, Peter. But somehow it didn't stop. It dragged on and on. All the time she was getting crazier and crazier about me. Then, one day, it all came to a head. She said she couldn't go on like that.

It was breaking her up having to share me. I had to tell Lottie and get a divorce."

Technically, I suppose, I felt sorry for him. With his vanity and foolish optimism, he had been such an easy victim for the Nanny-spider—a helpless male spider, destined, in true arachnid fashion, to be devoured by his mate. But my sympathy was tinged with contempt. The murderer, however boyish and charming, who kills through weakness and hides behind his best friend, is not the most attractive character in the world. No, when the time came to jump in and trip him up, it wasn't going to worry me.

". . . I was horrified, Peter. I mean, about the divorce thing. I—I tried to explain how impossible it would be. I owed everything to Lottie, I said. And not only that. Without Lottie, I wouldn't have a cent. She'd throw me right out, I said. How the hell could Nanny and I live on nothing?"

He was pacing up and down the room now, explaining how he had argued and pleaded with Nanny. As he told it, his guileless belief that everything would be all right just because he wanted it to be all right, had been almost incredible. He had really thought he had charmed her into respecting his comfortable berth with Lottie and forgetting all about the divorce. He had suspected no ulterior purpose when she had asked him to slip her into Lottie's party. He had even been naïve enough, after he had known she was cultivating me, not to speculate on her motives.

"I saw her all the time at Gordon's, after the party, Peter. And she did talk about some plan she had. But— I was dumb, I guess—I never linked up her plan with you. I suppose, back of my mind, I was hoping she'd switch to you and give me a let-out. For a while, I even kidded myself it would happen that way." The tip of his tongue came out to moisten his lip. "But, of course, I'd never made a bigger mistake in my life."

I was feeling very tense now, for, suddenly, it had occurred to me that his story wasn't going the way I had expected it to go. If he had merely wanted to give me a version of his relationship with Nanny which was convincing enough to explain away the use of Gordon's apartment, hadn't he already gone too far? Wasn't he coming dangerously near a point where he would incriminate himself without any help from me? Had I then completely misunderstood him? Had he, from the beginning, been planning a full confession?

"Peter—" his voice was awkward now—"do you think I should go on?"

"Why not, Brian?"

"I mean—this is strictly between you and me. You understand that, don't you?"

His expression was affectionate, almost foolishly convinced of our mutual sympathy and trust. I saw it all then. Of course I had misunderstood him! He was even more staggeringly stupid and conceited than I had imagined. He had found it painful to have to keep to himself the fact that he had murdered Nanny. He was welcoming an opportunity to get it off his chest. And I, of course, was the obvious father confessor—because I was a pal, a pal who had suffered as much as he had from Nanny Ordway, a pal who would be blithely prepared, out of friendship, to listen, to say "there-there-Brian" and, by keeping my mouth shut, to become an accessory after the fact.

For a moment I was staggered. Then I was pleased. It was going to be much easier than I had imagined. I wasn't going to have to try to trick him. All I had to do was to sit there and let him convict himself out of his own mouth.

"Sure, Brian," I said. "Of course I understand. This is strictly between you and me. Go on."

A relieved smile spread across his face. "Okay, Peter. I'll feel a lot better going the whole way. You see, it all came to a head the—the day she died. That morning, around noon, she called me from downstairs in your apartment. That was the first time she'd done it and I was scared about Lottie, but luckily Lottie was out at the photographer's. She said she had wonderful news. I was to come down right away. When I got there, she was radiant. I'd never seen her like it. She threw her arms around my neck. She said, 'It's all right, darling. All our problems are solved at last. My plan worked. I've fixed it.' I hadn't the slightest idea what she was talking about, Peter. I swear it. And when she explained, I could hardly believe it. I mean, I'd never dreamed a girl could be like that. You—you know, of course?"

I said, "She told you how she'd framed me?"

He nodded. "That and—and how she was pregnant. She told me that first and it pretty much threw me. A doctor'd done a test and it was positive. We were having a baby, she said. Wasn't that wonderful? She went on cooing about *our* baby before she told me about the other thing. Then I got it full in the face—how she'd planted the evidence against you with her roommate, with Gordon, with Lucia, with Iris—everything. 'It's a cinch,' she said. 'When the time comes, I'll slap a paternity suit on him. With all that proof, he's never going to take it to court. I'll get a great fat settlement. All we've got to do is wait a while. Then when I collect, you can divorce Lottie. We'll have enough money. We'll be able to live together with our baby.'"

Very quietly, he went on, "When I heard that, Peter, I thought she was a maniac. No, I didn't. Not really. I only saw I was caught, that she had turned out to be even stronger than Lottie, that she'd never let me go. I didn't want her. God knows, I didn't want any part of her. I tried to argue. I said it wouldn't be fair to you. She just laughed. Then I said it wouldn't be fair to Lottie, and she laughed again. 'That old bag,' she said. 'Who cares about that old bag?' That made me mad. I said I'd be damned if I'd go along with any such stinking scheme against my own best friend. She got mad too, then. She started yelling at me. 'Okay,' she said, 'if you're not grateful for all I've done, if you haven't the decency to stand by your own baby, let's respect your beautiful friendship with Peter Duluth. Let's stick to the real story. Let's slam it all over the headlines. *Charlotte Marin's Husband Fathers Young Girl's Baby.* That'd look pretty, wouldn't it? Lottie would love that, wouldn't she?"

He broke off. I could see it all as if I'd been there. The Nanny-spider out in the open at last—ready to devour her mate. Grudgingly, I thought: Poor devil. At least Nanny Ordway hadn't loved me. I had been spared that.

"Somehow, Peter, I went on stalling. I asked her at least to give me time to think. Finally she said okay, she'd give me till three o'clock. I was to come down again at three. And if I didn't agree by then . . ."

There was a sudden commotion in the hall. He broke off. We both sprang to our feet. Lottie came storming into the living-room, followed by Iris.

"Peter Duluth, what is this? What are you up to?"

She was wearing a black hat with an eye veil. It was an absurd hat, glamorous for someone else but not for Lottie. As she plunged, chattering, toward us, the breath from her words sent the little veil puffing out like a jib in a squall.

"The idea! Trying to fool me! The moment I saw Iris, I could tell she was furtive about something. Plotting, planning. Talking to Brian alone. What is it? What are you saying to Brian?"

Iris, pale and unhappy, joined me. "I'm sorry, Peter. It didn't work."

"Work! I'll say it didn't work."

Lottie had taken up her position squarely in front of Brian, gazing at me accusingly. I was angry and frustrated by her disastrously timed interruption. But, in spite of all that, I thought: What am I going to do with her? Half of me was still exasperated by her. She was an impossible woman; she'd done everything she could think of to bitch me and, just irritatingly, had gone on insisting she was my best friend. I shouldn't be giving a damn what happened to her now. It was her own nosiness that was defeating her.

But, somehow, Lottie was Lottie. You didn't expect her to be any different. I had to finish with Brian now. Everything depended on it. But I just couldn't bring myself to go it with Lottie right in the room, glaring up at me like a belligerent mother hen.

I said, "Lottie, won't you please go away?"

"Go away! And whose apartment is this supposed to be?"

"Yes, Lottie," said Iris. "Please. . . ."

"What is this?" Lottie swung around to Brian. "Brian, what are they doing?"

Brian looked as uncomfortable as I felt.

"It's nothing. It . . ."

The front door buzzer sounded. It was almost a relief. At least it made a distraction.

Iris said, "I'll go."

She went out into the hall. Lottie, Brian, and I stood around like very bad actors in a very bad play with no direction at all.

I could hear voices from the hall. Then Iris reappeared.

"It's . . ." she began.

But there wasn't any need for her to go on.

Lieutenant Trant came strolling after her into the room.

CHAPTER TWENTY

He was smiling his grave, ominous smile. He was exactly the way I had visualized he would be when he finally came to arrest me. I felt suddenly, ferociously angry with Lottie. Goddamn her, I thought. If she hadn't barged in, I'd have got the confession from Brian.

Now, of course, Brian would clam up. Now I had nothing.

Standing on the room's threshold, Lieutenant Trant was still maddeningly unpolicemanlike. He was the rather severe, rather elegant guest come to pay a social call. He should have cards printed up, I thought, and butlers should carry them in ahead of him on silver trays.

Lieutenant Trant—Executioner.

"Good evening," he said.

We were all looking at him with varying degrees of uneasiness. It was Lottie who took hold of the scene.

"What on earth are you doing here?"

"I'm afraid I don't bring very good news. Certainly it'll be a shock for some of you." He paused, deliberately, it seemed to me, ignoring my presence. "Nanny Ordway didn't commit suicide, Miss Marin. She was murdered."

I flashed a glance at Brian. He hadn't changed much. He just looked a little paler and tauter. Somehow his big white apron, which had seemed normal enough before, now looked silly and rather embarrassing.

Once again it was Lottie who held the stage.

"Murder!" she exclaimed. "What nonsense. What nonsense everyone's talking tonight."

"I'm sorry, Miss Marin. It isn't nonsense."

Trant was watching Brian now. Slowly, almost leisurely, he started to move toward him. "I apologize, Mr. Mullen, for my low habits, but this evening, when you and your wife were out to dinner, I had a microphone installed—" he gestured toward a semi-abstract portrait of Lottie—"right behind that picture. There's a recording machine up in Mr. Duluth's apartment. I've been sitting up there, listening to everything you've been telling him."

I was at sea now. A dictaphone in Brian's apartment! Why not in mine? Was it conceivable that Trant had changed his victim, that all this time when I'd thought the Law was pursuing me . . . ? No, I thought. It couldn't be that simple. Not with Trant. This was some kind of a trap.

Lottie was looking at him. She was very quiet now, but it was the quiet she used on the stage before she built to a big scene. Any minute, I knew, she was going to butt in. She was going to cause havoc with Trant before she was through.

Trant was still moving toward Brian. "You cleared up most of the things I was still doubtful about, Mr. Mullen. But, thanks to your wife's interruption, you didn't carry your story quite far enough, did you? You described your morning session with Nanny Ordway in Mr. Duluth's apartment. You admitted she had told you to go down again at three o'clock with your final decision. But that's where you stopped. You should have finished the story. You should have told Mr. Duluth how you went down at three, how she threatened once again to make your life impossible if you didn't fall in with her plans. You should have told him how you murdered her—as the only way to save your marriage."

I was listening with an extraordinary mixture of bewilderment and relief. So, for some improbable reason, Trant wasn't hounding me any more. He had the solution. There had been no need for my acrobatic attempts to save myself.

Iris had been standing beside me. Now, quickly, she crossed to Lottie. That made me, too, remember Lottie with a prick of alarm. I looked across at her. Her face was terrifying because it had become suddenly sagging and old. Ironically, I realized it would have been better for her if I'd told her before Trant arrived. This way she was having to swallow the bitter, bitter pill without any sugar-coating at all.

But Iris had her arm around her. I turned toward Brian. He was terribly shaken too. His face wore the dazed, almost beatific expression of a prize-fighter teetering on his heels just after a knock-out blow.

"Of course, Mr. Mullen—" Trant's quiet, penetrating voice was sounding again—"if you'd told Mr. Duluth all that, it would have been embarrassing to explain why you left the body in his apartment where it would certainly implicate him. But, after all, Mr. Duluth's an understanding man. He would have appreciated your problem. The body was there. You could hardly lug it away. At least you did your best to make it look like suicide—with the chandelier, the faked suicide note. . . ."

"But," gasped Brian, "but that wasn't it. That—that isn't true."

"It isn't?" snapped Trant. "You didn't go down to Mr. Duluth's apartment again at three o'clock?"

"No."

"Why not? She'd told you to go down, hadn't she?"

"Y-yes."

"But you didn't go?"

"I didn't go."

"Then at least she called you. When you didn't show up, she'd certainly have called you."

"Oh, yes." Brian seemed to be regaining a little control. "She called—around three-fifteen."

"And what did she say?"

"She asked why I hadn't come down. She—she said she hoped I was more sensible by then, that—" Brian's eyes shifted miserably to Lottie and then back again to Trant—"that I'd realized my place was with her and my baby and . . ."

"And—what?"

Brian crossed to Lottie. He took her hands in his, while she gazed up at him dully. "Lottie, if only I'd told you earlier, I could have explained. I could have made you understand. Now, please, don't get mad, not till I've had a chance to explain."

"Mr. Mullen," cut in Trant, "I'm waiting to hear what happened next. She called you; she threatened you again and—and what?"

Brian turned back from Lottie. His face was crimson now. "I wanted to tell her to go to hell. I'd have liked to do that more than anything in the world. But, all afternoon, I'd been sitting here, figuring, and I'd decided: What was the point of going against her? If I did, she'd tell Lottie." He gestured helplessly toward his wife. "Once Lottie knew, she'd throw me out. I knew, if I went against her, I'd lose everything. I guess I'm pretty much of a coward. If I'd had any guts, I'd have done something, but . . . I didn't. I didn't fight her. I didn't even try. I thought if—if I strung along with her, at least it would give me a couple of months. Something might always turn up, I thought. So that's what I told her on the phone. I said I'd let her go ahead and sue Peter; I'd stand by her; and when the time came I'd get a divorce. . . . I gave in all along the line. And it satisfied her. She said I wouldn't ever regret it, that—that she loved me. And she hung up."

He was looking down at the carpet. "That was all, Lieutenant. You're crazy to say I killed her. She hung up and I never saw her again. If you don't believe me, ask Lottie. She came in just after that—just about ten minutes later. I was here. She can prove that."

Trant had been listening with his own peculiar brand of silence which managed to question each statement and somehow make it seem improbable and false. His voice was implacable now.

"So that's how you claim it happened?"

"That's how it did happen."

"It isn't very plausible, is it? A girl was downstairs in that apartment, threatening to ruin you. You were up here. A few minutes later she was dead." He took a sudden step forward. "If you didn't kill her, who did?"

It was then that Brian looked straight at me. He didn't say anything, but his face, both puzzled and reproachful, was infinitely expressive.

"Tell me," Trant was repeating, "if you didn't kill her, Mr. Mullen, who did?"

It was then that Lottie moved. It was the slightest of movements, but I knew the trick so well from her acting. It was the first, deliberately small movement after complete stillness—and it always worked. It worked now. All of us, almost before we realized it, had turned to look at her.

She had her face back under control. She still looked too elaborate and over-glamorized in the terrible hat, but, behind the veil, her eyes were as clear, as gimlet sharp as ever. There was even the smile on her mouth which I knew so well. Around the theater, they called it her "watch-out" smile.

For a moment the gimlet gaze was settled on me. Then, very slowly, she turned it to Trant.

"All this is really true, Lieutenant? You're sure this—this little girl was murdered?"

Trant seemed as much under her spell as the rest of us.

"There isn't any doubt about it, Miss Marin."

"And you are honestly idiotic enough to accuse my husband?"

"There's plenty of evidence."

"Evidence! What sort of evidence? What sort—indeed?"

Suddenly she swung around to me. Her hand came out, pointing. It wasn't just a woman pointing. It was the mother in *Térese Raquin* pointing at her son's destroyer; it was Electra pointing Orestes up the steps toward Cassandra.

"There he is!" she exclaimed. "There is the murderer of Nanny Ordway."

The finger was still pointing as she turned to Trant. "From the start I've known it, but, fool that I was, I tried to protect him because he was my friend. That day, around three-fifteen, I came back from the photographer's. My new pictures were ready. I wanted them put up outside the theater that night. I stopped off at Peter's floor to tell him. I went to the door. I was going to knock. Then I heard voices—Peter's voice . . . a girl's voice. . . ."

She paused for the fraction of a second, then the beautiful voice in all its rich sonority boomed on:

"I heard the girl say: No . . . no . . . no . . . please! I stood there, with my hand up to the door. What is this? I thought. What's the matter? Then I heard Peter's voice. It was loud, fierce. 'I'll fix you,' he said. That's what he said. 'I'll fix you.' That's when I thought: This is not for me. I came up the stairs to the apartment. Brian was here. I found him right here in this room, reading the paper."

She moved to Brian and put her hand protectively on his arm.

"There, Lieutenant. There it is. That's all I have to say."

CHAPTER TWENTY-ONE

"Peter!"

Iris ran to my side. I was staring with shocked incredulity at Lottie. The bitch! I thought. She was perfectly serene now, standing there with her hand on her exonerated husband's arm, slightly lofty as if she had said her piece and was above any tiresome details that might still have to be settled.

There was the faintest trace of a smile on Trant's lips as he watched her. He was happy. Of course he was. His ruse had worked. Peter Duluth, the seducer, the liar, the cowardly murderer, was finally in the trap.

He said: "Miss Marin, you're prepared to come around to the station-house and make a sworn statement of what you've just said?"

"Naturally." Lottie, the grande dame, shrugged. "If it's necessary."

Very quietly, Trant said: "I don't recommend it, Miss Marin."

"You don't recommend it? Why not? Why ever not?"

Trant's smile was a real smile now, not just the suggestion of one. "Because I never recommend perjury."

"Perjury!" exclaimed Lottie.

"Yes, Miss Marin. Your story was very convincing, but there's one unfortunate hitch. You couldn't have heard Mr. Duluth in his apartment at three—because at three Mr. Duluth was at a movie."

"Pooh." Lottie waved an arm. "That's just what he says."

"That's what I thought, too, Miss Marin. But I'm afraid I made as much of a fool of myself as you. A couple of hours ago, one of my men brought in the boy who'd been collecting the tickets at the theater that afternoon. He'd been sick and we'd had difficulty locating him. But finally they brought him in."

Trant flashed me a glance out of the corner of his eye. That was the first time, since his arrival, that he'd paid me any attention at all.

"As it happens, Miss Marin, the ticket collector is a would-be actor. He's been around to all the producers' offices many times. The moment Mr. Duluth turned in his ticket at two-thirty, he recognized him. He recognized him again when he came out at four-thirty. There's no doubt about the day, either. Mr. Duluth has an alibi which nothing on earth can break."

It was only then that Lottie's godlike poise collapsed. Even though half of me was absorbed with the miracle of Trant, against all expectations, becoming my champion, I noticed it with grim satisfaction.

She had broken away from Brian, throwing out her hand in a feeble little gesture that meant nothing at all. For a moment, the silence was extreme. It was Iris who broke it. Her face was clouded with astonishment and shock.

"Lieutenant," she exclaimed, "did she make all that up about Peter?"

"I'm afraid she did."

"Of all the low-down, stinking . . ."

My wife lunged forward toward Lottie. Trant caught her arm.

"Now, Mrs. Duluth—please. . . ."

His voice was soft, almost paternal. Iris glanced back at me.

I said, "Let it go, baby."

"But, Peter . . ."

"Let it go."

She came back to my side, still seething with indignation. Trant turned to Brian.

"Okay, Mr. Mullen, you're under arrest."

"No!" cried Lottie.

Trant ignored her. There was a new harshness, a melodramatic quality to him which was quite unfamiliar to me. He was being the theatrical cop, something out of the movies, not at all the Lieutenant Trant I had known.

"You'll come with me, Mr. Mullen. And I don't advise you to make difficulties. I have men outside. They're armed. And . . ."

He felt in his pocket and tugged out a pair of handcuffs. Once again I was conscious of a false exaggeration of gesture. He grabbed at Brian's unresisting wrist. The handcuffs flashed as he brought them forward.

Lottie flew at him. "Don't! Don't do it!"

"Why not?"

"You can't."

"He's under arrest. You've interfered enough already."

"No."

Astonishingly Trant whipped around and grabbed her arms. "Why not? Why shouldn't I arrest him?"

"Because . . ."

"Because he didn't do it?"

"No, no. He didn't do it."

I'd never seen Lottie like that before. She had no dignity, no presence. She was just struggling blindly—like Miss Amberley quivering with terror in my grip.

Trant's voice was dominating, metallic. "Why didn't he do it, Miss Marin? How do you know?"

"I know. . . ."

"Because you killed her yourself! That's it—isn't it? You came home around three-fifteen. You let yourself into the hall. You heard your husband in here on the phone. You heard enough of what he was saying to make you curious. You tiptoed out to the kitchen. You picked up the extension. And you heard her—you heard Nanny Ordway downstairs. You heard her say: Your place is with me and my baby. And you heard your husband say: Yes, I admit it. I'll get a divorce."

Lottie, still held by the arms, had stopped struggling. But her passivity was almost worse than the hysterical violence that had gone before it. Her face was tilted up to Trant's. Her lips were half parted. She seemed hypnotized, unable to move, to think, to do anything but listen.

"Yes," Trant was saying, "that's how it happened. You listened. You put down the receiver. You went down by the backstairs. Your husband! you thought. The man that belonged to you! Your husband! That girl was trying to take him away from you. That girl was having a baby by him. You knocked on the door. She let you in. You said: I know all about you. I know it all. You're going to leave my husband alone. That's what you said. And she looked at you, didn't she? She looked at you and laughed. What do you think you can do about it? she said. He's mine. I'm having his baby. You think you can compete with me—an old bag like you?"

He threw the words straight at her white, stricken face. It was horrible but horribly vivid as if, by some uncanny trick, he had taken us all back into that room.

"Her scarf was there, wasn't it, Miss Marin? It was lying there, maybe over the back of a chair. Maybe she turned away from you, showing her contempt for you. You saw the scarf. . . . You were furious—furious, bewildered, frightened, hurt. You picked up the scarf, you . . ."

"No!" shouted Lottie suddenly. "No, no."

Trant's hands were still on her arms. "You deny it? You deny that's what happened? Then your husband will go to jail; he'll be tried; he'll be convicted. He'll be killed, Miss Marin. The man you committed murder for will be killed!"

"Stop." The word came from Lottie in a wrenching gasp. "Stop it, I say."

She twisted out of his grasp and ran to Brian, throwing herself against him.

"I'd known it," she cried. "For weeks I'd known there was someone. But I never realized it was she—that little slut, that scheming, sly, pale little slut. . . . She wasn't going to take you away from me."

The words choked into a sob. I saw with a kind of instinctive professional detachment that it was exactly like her stage sobbing—ugly, harrowing.

Trant's face was almost gray now. He moved across after her.

"All right, Miss Marin? You'll come with me?"

"You're mine," Lottie was babbling. "You're mine, Brian. You're all I've got."

"Miss Marin, you'll come with me to the station-house?"

She turned her head so that she could glance up at Trant. She gave an almost invisible nod.

Trant said to Brian, "You'd better take her in the bedroom. See she gets some things packed."

"But . . ."

"Do it."

Brian put his arm around his wife's waist and guided her into the next room. Trant watched them and then dropped down onto the arm of a chair. I saw that his hands were shaking.

It had happened so quickly, so unexpectedly that my thoughts were skittering around. But already I could see the inevitability of the motive. *Lottie owns Brian.* Miss Mills had said that. And it was the key to it all. You couldn't take anything from Lottie. No one could. Not even Nanny Ordway.

I looked at Trant. I saw now what his ruse had been and I felt a kind of awed admiration.

"You accused Brian from the beginning to try to force her to confess?"

He glanced up and nodded vaguely.

"And I thought . . ."

The corners of his mouth twisted in a slight smile. "That I was going to arrest you. I'm sorry, Mr. Duluth. I've got a lot of apologies to make to you."

"But how did you figure it out?"

"Once your alibi was confirmed, once I'd talked to Gordon Ling, it was easy enough to get on to Mr. Mullen's part of it. And then I thought—well, on the character side, I couldn't see Mr. Mullen as a killer, but . . ."

"You could see Lottie?"

"Yes. I could see Miss Marin."

And now that he had completed the puzzle, I could see it too. There had been an almost terrifying consistency in the pattern. Male spiders don't kill female spiders. Flies don't kill spiders, either. It had needed a worthy antagonist to kill Nanny Ordway. What are the spiders' mortal enemies? The wasps.

Lottie, the wasp, had destroyed the Nanny-spider.

I was still looking at Trant, thinking that I owed him as many apologies as he owed me. Nanny Ordway's dupe —that was what I'd thought of him. How wrong I had been!

"And that's all you had?" I asked. "Just that hunch?"

He threw out a hand. "I'm afraid I'm not that much

of a wizard, Mr. Duluth. No, I had evidence, but it wasn't really enough to stand on its own without a confession." He paused. "When I was first up here, I noticed a lot of doodles on the telephone pad. Even though I had you picked out as the murderer then, I don't like to let anything pass. I knew there'd be a question of drawing with the suicide note. So I picked them up and shipped them over to the expert. His report came back this evening. He's ready to go on the stand and testify that the doodles and the drawing of the hanged girl were made by the same person."

I thought back to the day when Lottie had picked up Nanny's drawing. The gimlet glance.

"Whatever is this?"

And all that was still muddled fell into place. Lottie Marin had killed Nanny Ordway as a passionately possessive woman fighting to keep what was hers. But to have killed is terrible and to go on living after you've killed is unendurable unless there is some support. Lottie had had the perfect support. She was an actress.

Most of her life both on and off the stage had been acting. How natural that, from the moment after the murder, the actress should have taken control. She must have known her only hope was to fake a suicide, and once she'd done it, once she'd torn off the title page of the story and doodled the hanged girl, once she'd somehow lugged the body up to the chandelier . . . Lottie Marin, the actress trained to believe her role, had already started to believe the suicide.

Probably, it had not been hard for her—because the role she had had to play from then on had been nothing but Lottie Marin—Lottie Marin swooping down to welcome Iris home, discovering the body, accusing me of driving "the poor little girl" to suicide, Lottie Marin doing and saying all the things that Lottie Marin would say and do.

And later, Lottie Marin hurtling to the theater with the red hot news, Lottie Marin rushing back to our apartment, commiserating with her "poor dear darlings," Lottie Marin shocked at the revelations of Lucia's sister, Lottie stoutly championing her best friend Iris against her shameful husband, Lottie Marin still being my best friend, Lottie indignant when I wouldn't play ball, Lottie Marin, in a final genius gesture of play-acting, flying into a tantrum and walking out of the show.

Yes, it had all been consistent. And it was wonderful in a way—even the magnificent shamelessness of that final pointing, accusing finger.

I felt a sudden, unreasonable sadness. Lottie had been the greatest actress of our time. There wouldn't be another Lottie, not in my day.

Trant had got up from the chair. Iris was hovering uncertainly at his side.

I said, "I guess you've got her now, Lieutenant. A confession in front of witnesses. . . ."

"Yes." He glanced at me and there seemed to be in his eyes a trace of my own regret. "Knowing what Nanny Ordway was—" He shrugged. "But I don't like murder, and I guess I've got this murderer."

My mind, racing forward into the future, was full of new speculations.

"I wouldn't be too sure."

"Not sure, Mr. Duluth?"

"Right now she's down. Wait till she's up again. Just wait till you see her at the trial. Before she's through, she'll have that jury carrying her out of the courtroom on their shoulders—cheering."

Lottie and Brian emerged from the bedroom. Brian was carrying a small case. Lottie didn't even look at us. She went right on to the door. Brian and Trant followed her.

For a moment Iris and I stood there together in silence.

Then we went down to our own apartment. I mixed us drinks. Neither of us said anything for quite a time. But gradually, with Lottie away, with the power of her personality fading, I came back to myself. I was Peter Duluth with a wife—Peter Duluth unexpectedly reprieved from the abyss.

And, because it's my nature to worry, I started to worry. Iris was sitting on the couch, pale and preoccupied. I crossed to her. I sat down next to her.

"Baby," I said, "you haven't signed with Alec, have you?"

She glanced up. "Signed? To go to England? Of course not. I didn't even like the play."

Slowly it was coming back to me—that wonderful, half-forgotten feeling that life was ordinary, that a day was just a day, that you wake up in the morning and there is your wife and you have your breakfast and you . . .

"Peter." She twisted around on the couch, her face still grave and reflective. "I've been thinking."

"Yes?"

"Miss Mills says the part in *Let Live* would be fine for me."

The feeling of life re-established was growing, swelling. It was wonderful.

"Do it," I said. "Do it, baby. It'd be perfect for you. And it would thrill Thomas Wood."

She was in my arms, clinging to me. Swedenborg and his two halves of the same soul.

"That's what we want, Peter. That's it, isn't it? We want to thrill Thomas Wood."

THE LIBRARY OF CRIME CLASSICS®

FRED ALLEN
Treadmill to Oblivion

CHARLOTTE ARMSTRONG
The Balloon Man
The Chocolate Cobweb
A Dram of Poison
Lemon in the Basket
A Little Less Than Kind
Mischief
The Unsuspected
The Witch's House

JACQUELINE BABBIN
Bloody Soaps
Bloody Special

GEORGE BAXT
The Affair at Royalties
The Alfred Hitchcock Murder Case
The Dorothy Parker Murder Case
I! Said the Demon
The Neon Graveyard
A Parade of Cockeyed Creatures
A Queer Kind of Death
Satan Is a Woman
Swing Low Sweet Harriet
The Talullah Bankhead Murder Case
Topsy and Evil
Who's Next?

KYRIL BONFIGLIOLI
Don't Point That Thing At Me
Something Nasty in the Woodshed

Nine—and Death Makes Ten
The Peacock Feather Murders
The Plague Court Murders
The Punch and Judy Murders
The Reader Is Warned
The Red Widow Murders
The Skeleton In the Clock
The Unicorn Murders
The White Priory Murders

HENRY CECIL
Daughter's In Law
Settled Out of Court

LESLIE CHARTERIS
Angels Of Doom
The First Saint Omnibus
Getaway
Knight Templar
The Last Hero
The Saint in New York

EDMUND CRISPIN
The Case of the Gilded Fly

CARROLL JOHN DALY
Murder from the East

LILLIAN DE LA TORRE
Dr. Sam: Johnson, Detector
The Detections of Dr. Sam: Johnson
The Return of Dr. Sam: Johnson, Detector
The Exploits of Dr. Sam: Johnson, Detector

PETER DICKINSON
Perfect Gallows
The Glass Sided Ants' Nest
The Sinful Stones

Headed for a Hearse
The Lady in the Morgue
Murder In the Madhouse
The Search for My Great Uncle's Head
Red Gardenias
Solomon's Vineyard

VICTORIA LINCOLN
A Private Disgrace
Lizzie Borden by Daylight

MARGARET MILLAR TITLES
An Air That Kills
Ask for Me Tomorrow
Banshee
Beast in View
Beyond This Point Are Monsters
The Cannibal Heart
The Fiend
Fire Will Freeze
How Like An Angel
The Iron Gates
The Listening Walls
Mermaid
The Murder of Miranda
Rose's Last Summer
Spider Webs
A Stranger in My Grave
Vanish In An Instant
Wall of Eyes

BARRY MALZBERG
Underlay

WILLIAM F. NOLAN
Look Out for Space
Space for Hire

WILLIAM O'FARRELL
Repeat Performance

STUART PALMER
The Penguin Pool Murder

STUART PALMER & CRAIG RICE
People VS Withers and Malone

BARBARA PAUL
Liars & Tyrants & People Who Turn Blue

ELLERY QUEEN
Cat of Many Tails
Drury Lane's Last Case
The Ellery Queen Omnibus
The Tragedy of X
The Tragedy of Y
The Tragedy of Z

PATRICK QUENTIN
Black Widow
Puzzle for Players
Puzzle for Puppets
Puzzle for Wantons

S.S. RAFFERTY
Cork of the Colonies
Die Laughing

DAMON RUNYON
Trials and Tribulations

CLAYTON RAWSON
Death from a Top Hat
Footprints on the Ceiling
The Headless Lady
No Coffin for the Corpse